I WAS COMPLETELY ENTHRALLED WITH THIS STORY!
I remember feeling like it was actually prophetic the first time
I read it. I appreciate how your characters develop and mature
throughout the years. Each one of them is so real and unique. The
introduction of the psychologist's explanation regarding how we
as humans process trauma was so good!

Set in Alberta and introduced by our native peoples perspective
immediately welcomed me into a story of overcoming a
catastrophe that affected the world on a global scale. The realistic
development of how man's inhumanity towards man may be
explained yet never excused captured my attention immediately.
The concept of consequences, both positive and negative, unfolds
with the voice of a true storyteller. **COULD NOT PUT IT DOWN!!!**
Susan Morris-Smith

**A VERY TIMELY AND EMOTIONALLY POWERFUL TALE OF THE
INDOMITABLE WILL OF THE HUMAN SPIRIT.** The author brings to
life memorable characters and draws you into their world as they
struggle to survive, dealing with the consequences of choices
made by them or for them. A definite page turner!
T Kapicki

ALSO BY
GAIL GILLINGHAM WYLIE
(PUBLISHED AS GAIL GILLINGHAM)

AUTISM

- Autism Handle with Care
- Autism A New Understanding
- Just So Happy, A Journey to Understanding Autism

SELF-HELP

- In Search of Self,
  A Personal Journey of
  Understanding and Acceptance

CONSEQUENCES

GAIL GILLINGHAM WYLIE

Cover photo "Prairie Morning" by Second Wind
secondwind.smugmug.com
Images by Steve Mumert

Published by Gail Gillingham Wylie, Edmonton, Canada

ISBN:
    Paperback   978-1-77354-542-4
       ebook   978-1-77354-543-1

Publication assistance by

PAGEMASTER
PUBLISHING
PageMaster.ca

PROLOGUE

"Behold our land."

Joseph Russell stood at the edge of the cliff, looking down at the forest spread out before him, as far as his eyes could see. He clutched his grandfather's hand tightly as he gazed, secure in the knowledge that he was safe. "It's so big....so big", he whispered. "And it's all ours?" He glanced up at his grandfather for confirmation.

"Grandpa, why are you crying?"

"See those trucks down there."

Joseph peered down in the direction that his grandfather was pointing. "On that little grey patch?"

"Yes, that one. Do you know what they are doing?"

"No."

"They are building a dam, a big dam."

"But it looks so tiny."

"Yes, it looks tiny now, but it is not going to stay that way.

"It's going to get bigger. When it gets big enough, it is going to stop the water from running. The dam will create a lake. A huge lake that will cover all the forest that you see before us; all of the land that our people have been living on for thousands of years. All of it will be under water. That's why I am crying. I brought you here to bid farewell to our land. I brought you here so that you can understand what we have lost; what has been stolen from us."

"But why would they want to do this?"

"They are going to use the dam to make electricity, enough electricity to give everyone lights. Enough electricity to run all our stoves and our fridges and televisions. They say there will be enough electricity created by this dam that it will supply all of this province and the province next to us. The white people need the electricity. They will steal our land to have it. They say that the three hundred and fifty thousand acres of prime forest that will be wiped out by this dam are worth it."

He gave a shuddering sigh and wiped his cheek with the back of his hand.

"When I was five, my grandfather brought me to this very spot to show me our land. It was the first lesson in so many he taught me about how important it is to take care of this beautiful world we live in, with all the gifts it provides. I brought you here today for the same reason. He spoke those same words to me that I said to you. Behold our land.' This part of the lesson has changed, but you will still need all the others. You will not inherit this land. It has been stolen from us. In the midst of this, we are a strong people. We will survive. Today I make this promise to you. I will pass on all the tools that my grandfather gave me. In time you, too, will do the same for your grandchildren."

1

TUESDAY

"Things always happen in threes." Grandmother's voice in her head drowned out that of the school secretary coming through the phone. Margret shook her head slightly, trying to clear her mind and make sense of what the woman was saying. Something about Marisa. Something about being attacked. Something about her needing to come to the school right away. It didn't make any sense. The secretary sternly repeated the words "We need you here as soon as you can make it". Automatically she replied, "yes, I'm on my way," and replaced the receiver on its base. She grabbed her keys off the hook and pulled her jacket out of the closet.

It only took a couple of minutes for Margret to back out of the driveway and head towards the school. Now that she was on the move, she was surprised at how swiftly she was reacting. This wasn't really like her. She had always been the cautious one; the one who waited for someone else to take control; the one who preferred to stay in the background, unnoticed by those around her; the one who worked out what she was going to do, slowly and carefully before she made any move. It didn't seem possible in the moment. Her daughter was in trouble, and she couldn't turn to John. He was somewhere, up in the air. She was going to have to look after this all on her own. Maybe this is what it feels like to be a Mama bear, she thought. I can do things if I need to.

The day had started out well. She woke up earlier than usual and decided to surprise the family with a breakfast of bacon, scrambled eggs and blueberry pancakes. As the smells wafted through the house, the whole family joined her in the kitchen without needing her to urge them out of bed. This gave them time to sit around the table and chat about the coming week in a way that was rare. John even had the time to drive the girls to school.

Margret sat at the table after they left, treasuring the picture of the family gathered for breakfast, with a smile on her face. This is what life is supposed to be like, she thought to herself. This is what makes having the freedom to be a stay home mother worthwhile.

It didn't last long. Shortly after John arrived at his office, he called to say that Nick was sick, and that he would have to take his place reporting on the pregame coverage of the Super Bowl. He would be flying out within a couple of hours and wasn't certain if he would be back before the Super Bowl was over. This was the biggest event that the sports magazine he worked for covered and they couldn't afford to miss anything. He would call again, once he was in his hotel, to let her know exactly where he was staying and how to reach him if his cell phone was turned off. Who knows, he might even know how long he would have to stay there by evening. It all depended on what was going on with Nick and how willing the editor was, to spend more money sending Nick down to replace him once he felt better.

The joy of family togetherness evaporated very quickly. Margret began to clear away the breakfast dishes with a heavy heart. She didn't like to be alone. Ever since her parents had died in the car crash and she had been sent to live with her grandmother in northern Alberta, she felt a huge hole in her abdomen whenever she was left alone. It wasn't bad during the day when the girls were at school and John was at work. She knew they would be back with her in late afternoon and there was plenty in the home and yard to keep her busy. But now John wouldn't be coming home for who knows how long.

Suddenly she clearly heard her grandmother voice. "This too shall pass." Yes, she thought to herself. It only will be a couple of weeks at the most. And the girls will keep me company. We can get through this. She focussed on the excitement in John's voice at the thought of being able to be at the Super Bowl. Nick was the senior reporter in the office and so he always got these plum assignments. Now John had his chance. She certainly couldn't deny him that. The stress in her abdomen began to subside.

The phone rang again. This call was even harder to take. It was a solicitor calling from Grande Prairie. After he introduced himself, he explained that he hated to give her this news on the phone. However, as the sole beneficiary of her grandmother's estate, she needed to be aware that her grandmother had been found dead in her bed by a neighbour. It appeared that she had died peacefully in her sleep. He went on to explain that there were a lot of decisions that had to be made. He, as the executor of the will, needed to know what provisions she wanted to make for a funeral and burial, as well as what she wanted to do with the home and all its contents. He was willing to wait until she could arrive in Grande Prairie, but he hoped that she would get there quickly. With shaking hands, she wrote down his name and phone number and told him she would get back to him in the morning. This wasn't something that she could deal with on her own. She needed John. She would tell him he would have to come home when he called tonight. It might not be fair to him, but what else could she do?

Margret was deep in thought about her grandmother when the phone rang again. She had only been ten when the accident robbed her of her parents, and she was sent to live with her. Grandma was a tough, self-sufficient woman who had raised her son on her own after her husband was killed in an accident in the oil patch. She worked as a legal secretary while he was growing up and had moved on to a job in the courthouse by the time Margret arrived on her doorstep. She had welcomed her granddaughter into her home with open arms and had done her best to assuage the grief the child was feeling. Grandma had never been able to completely replace her parents, but she had been as solid as a rock throughout Margret's life. She was someone who she could depend upon completely; share feelings with openly; and, who she knew had her back, no matter what she chose to do.

It had been hard to leave her grandmother's home after she graduated from high school, but Grandma had insisted that she get a university education. She was in her third year of her Bachelor of Arts when she met John. He was a fledging reporter at the time, travelling across the country writing stories about different universities. It was love at first sight, on her part, when she saw him sitting in the cafeteria of the residence that she lived in. She couldn't believe her luck when he looked up at her and motioned her to join him at the table. It didn't take long for her to realize that all he was interested in was getting another interview with a student under his belt, but she was delighted to find him so easy to talk to. Even so, she was shocked to hear herself asking him if he was interested in accompanying her to the street dance in front the of the student's union building that evening. He replied "yes". As they spent that evening together a bond was formed that had only grown stronger over the years. He did leave the following week to write about another university, but they remained close through phone calls and e-mails as she completed her degree and started a job working with the local paraplegic association.

In time, John was offered a job at the sports magazine in Minneapolis and they decided they should get married. Moving so far away from Grandma was difficult but she insisted that Margret not worry about her. She could still see the smile on her grandmother's face as she said, "When you have found the man who has your heart, you must be with him, no matter where he goes. I had that love with your grandfather. I will never regret it. That's why I have never remarried. He was the love of my life. He gave me your father, who in time gave me you. Such gifts I can never regret. Now you have it with John. Go with my blessing and build your life together. I will be okay."

And so, she did. The years flew by. In the beginning she made sure that they saw each other at least once a year. Grandma flew down to spend a couple of weeks with the family after the births of both of their daughters. But as she aged, traveling began to get a little more difficult for her. It was now Margret's turn to get on the plane and fly north. Sadly, as her the girls grew older and became involved with more and more activities, there wasn't as much time available. The visits began to get further and further apart. It had been three years since Margret found the time for her grandmother. And now it was too late.

The tears began to quietly flow down Margret's cheeks as she drove towards the school. Scenes of her grandmother's face flashed through her mind: laughing out loud as they twirled in the tea cups at Disneyland; solemn, yet relaxed while listening to a sermon; frustrated as she showed her the damage done to the cabbages by the cutworms in the garden; intent as she studied the letter tiles in front of her, trying to come up with the best combination of letters that fit on the Scrabble Board. Such a dear face! How could she live without it? She reached for a Kleenex to wipe away the tears, thinking that she really shouldn't be driving in this condition. But what else could she do?

The sight of the line of police cars parked in front of the school slammed into Margret's body. Gasping for air, she managed to pull over to the curb and slip the car into park. Her head dropped down onto the steering wheel as she fought to regain her composure. Not this, not now – it was too much to take.

She was thankful that she knew what was happening to her. But, at the same time, she didn't know if she was strong enough to deal with it, along with everything else. She was in the midst of a flashback. A little girl standing in the front entrance of her school as the social worker gently told her that she had to come with her; that her parents had been in a car accident; that everything would all right. Meanwhile the lights on the police car outside the school flashed continuously. The police car that had brought this woman into her life.

Margret had started going to a psychiatrist shortly after she turned forty because she was experiencing panic anxiety attacks. Together, she and Dr. Perrson had explored what triggered these attacks and how best to deal with them. He had assured her that she was all right and that these attacks were actually flashbacks to the time she lost her parents. They were the body's way of releasing the emotions that she had not been safe to feel at that time. They were brought on by sensory input: smells, sounds, and/or sights which matched those she experienced as a child. She had learned to allow herself to sink into the feelings when they happened and to release the stored emotions. And she was kind of proud of how well she was getting at responding. But not now. Not when she had so much to deal with. Not when Marisa needed her. She began to breathe deeply and allowed the confusion of the young child to sweep through her body.

A tap on the window brought her back to the present. She sat up and looked into the concerned face of a police officer who asked, "Are you all right?"

Margret pressed the button to open the window as she silently nodded. It took a few seconds to find her voice.

She stammered. "My daughter.......". A shudder ran though her body as a sob escaped. "My grandmother. My parents. It's all too much."

"Well I don't know about the other members of your family, but I do know your daughter is okay. All of them are. A little shook up, if she was part of the group, but she is going to be fine."

"What happened?" Margret raised her hands to her head and pressed both sides of her skull. "The school secretary phoned, but I couldn't make head or tail of what she was saying. I just got word that my grandmother died, you see, and everything was fuzzy. Nothing was making any sense to me. She told me I had to come, so I did."

"Well, I think we had better get you inside and find your daughter. I don't know all the details so we'll wait until they can tell you everything there. Do you think you can walk?"

Margret nodded and opened the door as the officer stepped back to give her room. She swung her feet out of the car and unsteadily got to her feet. The weakness didn't surprise her. It was all part of these flashbacks. She reached out to the policewoman without hesitation saying, "I think you had better help me. I'm not feeling very steady in the moment".

As the two women walked arm in arm together towards the entrance of the school, Margret shared her experience of losing her parents with the officer. Dr. Perrson had stressed how important it was to get everything out in the open during these episodes and Margret had learned how powerful it was in the past. She told her about the police coming to the school with the social worker who told her about her parents. She told her about the first flashback which happened when a police car was parked in front of a neighbor's house with the lights flashing. She told her about feeling numb; of not being able to cry, even when she had to stay with the social worker until her grandmother arrived. As the words poured out of her mouth, she wondered if the officer was even slightly interested in what she was saying. It didn't matter. What mattered was that Margret needed to be strong for her daughter. Talking about her childhood memories would help. It had to be done, no matter who was walking beside her.

It did help. As the words flowed, so did the energy throughout her body. Step by step, she could feel her legs gradually regaining their strength.

The principal was waiting at the entrance of the school as they approached. "Mrs. Ashton, I'm so glad you made it. Is John coming?"

"No, he's on an airplane right now, heading off to his next assignment."

"Okay, then you're the last. We can get started. Come with me."

He turned and walked down the hallway to the open door of the music room with Margret close behind. As they entered the room, Margret could see several parents and students seated in the row of chairs that faced the lectern. Marisa was sitting beside her best friend Teri, but as soon as she saw her mother she got up and rushed towards her.

They hugged each other tightly and then stepped back and sat down, side by side, as the principal began to speak.

"I am just going to give a brief description of what has happened. I expect that your daughters will be able to tell you more once you get them home. They are all a bit shaken, which is to be expected, so we are excusing them from their classes for the rest of the afternoon. To summarize, these five students have a study period together just before lunch. Today they decided to leave the school early and go to Burger King to eat. As luck would have it, one the girls, Jeanne, remembered that she had left her money in her locker and turned back to get it. She told the others to keep going. She would catch up with them. As they rounded the corner, which cuts off the view of the school, they were suddenly accosted by a group of young men who drove up in three black cars, blocking the street. These men got out of the cars and encircled the girls, taunting them, calling them names and within minutes grabbed each of them and pulled them towards the cars. Jeanne saw this, as soon she came around the corner. She turned and headed back to the school, calling 911 as she ran. A police car was nearby and rushed to the location with its siren going. As soon as the men heard the siren, they let go of the girls, jumped in the cars and drove off."

"As you can see, our girls did put up a pretty good fight." The principal pointed to the bruise on Marisa's cheek and her torn jacket sleeve. "Thankfully, Jeanne wasn't with them. We don't know what would have happened if she been there too."

Tears sprang to Margret's eyes as she looked at the bruise on Marisa's face. She had been so focused on finding out why she was here, she hadn't even noticed it. She reached up her hand to gently touch it and murmured, "My poor baby."

"It's okay, Mom", Marisa whispered and dropped her head down on Margret's shoulder for a moment. Then they both turned their attention back to the principal.

"At this moment we have turned everything over to the police. They are going to want to interview each of the girls individually today and then you can all go home. Each girl has been assigned a couple of officers for the interviews. They will take place here in the school rather than going to the station, which is why there are so many cars outside. The police need you parents to be present during the interviews." "But before we do that, are there any questions?"

One of the fathers raised his hand. "Do you think that this has anything do to with the white slavery movement that we have been hearing so much about on the news?" A murmur ran through the room. This man had put the thoughts that everyone was holding in the back of their minds, right out into the open.

A policeman, who had been standing at the back of the room, walked forward, turned to face the group, and said, "it's a possibility. We can't say so for certain at this point, but we will definitely be investigating that angle, along with others." He looked directly at Jeanne and smiled. "Maybe your forgetfulness will be the big break that we need in this case." He turned and surveyed the whole group again. "Anything else?"

This time it was one of the mothers who raised her hand. Her voice trembled as she asked, "If they had taken the girls, what would they have done with them?"

The police man looked directly at her and answered in a soft voice, "We have no idea. We don't know who they are and we don't want to waste our time speculating on what they were thinking." His eyes swept the room. "Right now, we want to ensure we get all the information we can while it is still fresh in the girls' minds. I suggest we break now and work with each of you on an individual basis."

The principal walked over to the door and opened it. Five police officers strode into the room, each holding a card. One by one they read out the name of one of the girls who had been attacked and then escorted them out of the room with their parents. Marisa's name came last and the principal said, "You can stay here for the interview." He turned and left the room with the policeman who had been talking to the group.

The officer that had accompanied Margret into the school entered the room. Together she and another officer set up a table and placed four chairs around it. She laid a compact recorder on the table and turned it on. The other officer brought legal note pads and pens out of his briefcase and arranged them on the table. Margret and Marisa followed the lead of the police officers moving to the chairs they had left empty. The interview was about to begin.

The room was quiet except for the soft voices of the officer asking questions and Marisa answering them. You could hear the scratch of the pen as every word was documented onto the legal pads. Margret tried desperately to follow what was going on, but she wasn't able to. This, too, was a common problem when she experienced a flashback. Making her brain focus on anything for more than a few seconds was impossible. It was as if a grey fog had enveloped her whole being. She closed her eyes and allowed herself to sink into the fog. Marisa was safe. The police would look after her. She didn't need to know the details at this moment. That would come later.

The arrival of a forensic team brought her back to the present. She learned that the reason that Marisa had the bruise on her face was because she had scratched the arm of the man who had tried to drag her to the car and he had slapped her in return. Each of her fingernails were carefully scraped. The DNA found in these scrapings may prove to be of major significance in the arrests of these men.

Once the forensic unit was finished Marisa was handed the statement that the police had documented and asked to read through it. "Were there any errors?"

"No."

"Was anything omitted that she wanted to add?"

"No."

They handed her a pen and showed her where to sign her name. Margret followed suit, signing her name as parent. The interview was over.

As they were ushered down the hallway, Margret paused for a moment, and then asked to speak to the principal. They turned around and went into his office. There she told him about the death of her grandmother who lived in northern Alberta. She admitted that she didn't know quite what she was doing. Everything had happened so fast, but she felt she should also take Joelle home with her. He approved, suggesting that girls bring their books home with them in case they didn't return to the school in the morning. Margret nodded in agreement. This was a good decision. She was glad that others were helping her find her way.

2

FRIDAY

Margret opened her eyes slowly, still lost for a moment in the world of dreams. The profile of her daughter's face, softened by the blur of the passing prairie behind her, filled her view and jolted her awake. "I'm sorry darling," she whispered "I didn't mean to doze off. I should be keeping you company."

Marisa kept her eyes firmly on the road ahead of her as she replied "It's okay Mom. I'm doing fine. There's not much traffic to worry about and the road is straight and even. Not much of a challenge, really."

"You're right, of course, but I know how boring it can be. It's better if you have someone to talk to." She glanced into the rear seat to see Joelle curled up under a blanket, fast asleep. "Neither of us seem of much use to you."

"You don't have to worry about me Mom. It's actually been nice to have this time alone to think about everything that has happened these last few days. It's been crazy since the incident at school; finding out about Grandma; packing up to head north; and, helping you make all the arrangements so that we can be gone for who knows how long. I've been enjoying the peace and quiet."

Margret straightened up and stretched, yawning as she did so. "I agree. It's been a crazy week. That's likely why I fell asleep so quickly."

"That and the fascinating scenery we are passing through, I'm sure," Marisa added. "It's guaranteed to put most people to sleep." She waved her hand towards the snow-covered fields on either side of the road.

Margret chuckled and then replied "Yes, but it's more likely because of that lunch I ate in Brandon. I'm afraid I made a pig of myself. Haven't had poutine for so long." Margret yawned again as she looked out the window on her right. "Where are we?"

"We've crossed the border into Saskatchewan and passed a small town called Moosomin. I thought about stopping and getting a photo at the Welcome to Saskatchewan sign but you both were sleeping so soundly I decided not to. Moosomin? What kind of a name do you think that is?"

"Probably Cree, or whatever language the local tribe speaks here. Many of the towns and cities in Canada have names like that from the past."

Margret reached down and pulled a map out of the pocket on the door. She studied it carefully. "How are you doing, driving wise? I can take over if you want".

"No, Mom, I'm kind of enjoying this. You can relax." "Okay." She went back to the map in her hand. "Let's see, the next big city is Regina. That's a little over two hours from here. Do you think you can make it that far? I can take over before we get in the city."

"Sounds great Mom. We'll probably have to stop for gas and a pee break by then anyway. But in the meantime, don't worry about me. I've got this!"

Margret smiled and leaned her head back against the head rest. I got this. She wasn't sure of how she managed to raise such independent daughters. She could never remember a time when she truly felt like she could say, I got this and mean it. Maybe they had skipped back a couple of generations and taken all their genes from their grandmother. She glanced to her left again at Marisa. How thankful she was that she had insisted that she be allowed to try out for her driver's licence as soon as she was old enough to have one. It was so much easier to make this trip with two drivers instead of one.

Margret closed her eyes and allowed her thoughts to drift back over the events of the past week. The tortured hours of pacing the floor after they had returned home from the school, waiting for John to call. Finally, his face appearing on the iPad: solid, dependable, and comforting. Her sobs as she begged him to come home on the next flight. His promise to her that he would try. The night of fitful sleep filled with dark images of men grabbing her daughters and driving off with them in a black van, only to have them reappear at her side with her grandmother. A much younger and more vibrant grandmother than she had seen in years. John's call the next morning when he asked to speak with Marisa. The agonizing minutes in the next room, biting her fingernails, as she waited to hear what they were talking about. And then finally, the family call in which John carefully explained that he could not leave right away. He wanted them to drive to Grande Prairie in the Dodge Caravan, taking as little with them as possible.

He would join them in Grande Prairie by air as soon as the Super Bowl was over. When Margret resisted, it was Marisa who took over the conversation, insisting that she would help drive and make sure they got to her grandmother's in record time.

They spent the next couple of days organizing for the trip. Since they weren't quite certain how long they would need to get everything accomplished once they reached Grande Prairie, they decided to give themselves a month. This should provide enough time to make the drive, arrange the funeral and to sort and pack everything that Margret wanted to bring back to the States with her. It would also give John the time to finish up his assignment at the Super Bowl so that he could fly up and join them for the drive back home.

Planning to leave for a month meant that the girls had to arrange to bring the school work they would miss along with them. They spent a day at school while Margret made sure the caravan was trip worthy. New tires were installed, an oil change was completed and the antifreeze in the radiator refilled. Hours were spent on the phone with the various people who would be affected by their absence: the lawyer in Grande Prairie, members of the various committees she was involved with, as well as the coaches of the sports teams that the girls belonged to. She had cancelled the newspaper deliveries and hired a handyman to ensure the walks were kept clean in case it started to snow. Her final step was to ensure that all the bills were paid up to date.

These were all tasks that John would have taken care of if he had been at home. She felt a small surge of pride as she realized she had managed to do it all on her own. She hoped that nothing had been forgotten. If it had, it would just have to wait until they returned.

She opened her eyes and watched the snow-covered prairie passing by. She was back in Canada, but it was going to be a Canada without her grandmother. Tears began to slip silently down her cheeks as she considered her reality. Taking responsibility had only just begun.

3

THURSDAY

Sheldon Robinson strode down the centre corridor of the departure area of the airport with a smile on his lips, dodging harried travelers and their suitcases with an easy fluid motion and grace that felt remarkable. He rarely entered this part of the airport because of the congestion one had to deal with, but today was different. It was his last day on the job and he was determined to make the best of it. He was so ready to celebrate. No one was going to take away the joy and anticipation he was feeling.

Sheldon reached up to touch his breast pocket where the crinkle of paper ensured him that his plane ticket was still there. He smiled. Jamaica! He was actually going to Jamaica. And then, as he thought about the money that was about to be deposited his bank account, his smile broadened. He wasn't only going to be in Jamaica, he was going there with enough money to do anything he wanted.

Sheldon glanced at the people passing him as he shifted the weight of the lunch bucket from his right to his left hand. He was sure they were oblivious to his presence. After all, who pays any attention to someone wearing a maintenance coverall in an airport? Tomorrow it would be different. Tomorrow he would be the one wearing new clothes and pulling his suitcase behind him, just like they were. He would be one of them.

But first he had to get through this day. He swung to the right and pushed open the employee's only door. As he stashed the lunch bucket in his locker, he thought about what he was going to eat for lunch. There were so many different choices available in the airport food court and today he planned to make the most of them. He patted the lunch box softly. "I'll be back for you later" he murmured. "Just sit tight."

The day flew by much more quickly than he had anticipated. The airport was going through its five-year recommissioning process and his current supervisor had assigned him to takes notes while he performed the quality control tests on the system of waterlines throughout the building. Walking through the building behind the supervisor, jotting down the numbers and notes on the clipboard was so much easier than many of the other tasks he could have had to do today.

Sheldon also didn't mind hanging out with Harry, a jovial man who had worked at the airport since it first opened. Totally competent, Harry was relaxed as he performed each test. He spent as much time describing, in detail, the plans he had for his life following his upcoming retirement in the spring, as he did on the tests he was performing. Sheldon had no trouble agreeing that the deep-sea fishing trips and lazy days lying in the sun on the beach were so much more enjoyable than slaving away at the airport every day. In the midst of this, he kept quiet about his own plans and held in his own joy and anticipation in check.

What Harry did not realize was that Sheldon wasn't going to have to wait until spring. His freedom from this job started the next morning.

Throughout the day Sheldon reminisced about the journey that had led him to this point. He had been abandoned by his father before birth and handed over to social services at age three by his mother. Sheldon had grown up in a series of different foster placements and group homes, none of which had worked out well. He was an angry and troubled child who never felt like he fit in anywhere.

This all changed when he and his best friend burst into the city library one afternoon, when he was fifteen. They were planning to create a major ruckus. Instead, the security guard at the door had grabbed their arms and ushered them to a back room where a meeting was in progress. There, about a dozen boys much like him, were sitting on chairs in a semicircle facing a small thin man who was speaking quietly. This man looked directly at them with piercing black eyes for a few seconds, then silently motioned them to take the two remaining chairs. He went on speaking as if he had never been interrupted. Sheldon's life took on a new course in a matter of minutes.

In the years that followed Sheldon discovered that Pierce Paxton was a man with a purpose. He claimed that he had grown up on the streets like many of the boys who were listening to him. He said it took one man to change his life, a man who had taken him in and given him a purpose in life. This man was a chemist who had spent his life dedicated to the goal of finding ways to heal the body. He had taken Pierce off the streets when he was only eight and given him a job cleaning his laboratory. Over the years Pierce had managed to graduate from high school and earn a university degree in psychology but he still found time to work alongside his benefactor in the laboratory. When he wasn't in the laboratory, he focussed his time reaching out to boys who were stuck in bad situations much like he had been as a child. The library offered him this conference room as a free space to spend with the boys. His goal was to give them the tools to make them self-reliant as adults.

Sheldon had forgotten that the topic of that day was the importance of holding on to one's self-respect, in the midst of any situation one had to deal with. The actual words held little meaning for him at the time. The power was in the voice. It only took a few minutes before he was completely mesmerised by the voice. He found himself unable to get up and leave the room while Pierce was speaking. Over the following weeks he also discovered he was powerless to resist going back for more.

Sheldon became a changed man. His days of being a rebel and fighting the system were over. He started to apply himself in school in ways that shocked his both his teachers and his social workers. He stopped roaming the streets at night and spent his free time reading the great novels of the world that Pierce advised him to read. But most of all, he attended the meetings in the library consistently, concentrating on every word spoken and trying to implement the principles Pierce taught. When he graduated from high school, Pierce was there in the crowd cheering him on. And when he told Pierce he didn't know what he wanted to do as a job, it was Pierce who pulled a few strings and got him into this position at the in the maintenance department of the airport, without any experience to speak of. He also arranged a small apartment nearby for him to live in.

That was four years ago. He would never forget those first few weeks on the job. He'd felt totally and completely lost most of the time. He didn't know anything and there was so much to learn. However, the other fellows on the crew were a good lot and showed him the way.

So much had changed since then. There wasn't a corner of the airport that he hadn't worked in at one time or another. There wasn't a single job he was assigned that he couldn't do. He took a lot of pride in his position and in his workplace, but it wasn't quite enough. So, when Pierce showed up at the apartment last week, he had been delighted to see him. And when he asked him to do a certain task for him, he responded immediately in the affirmative.

Pierce didn't explain further. He said the tools and instructions would be delivered later. All Sheldon had to do was carry them out as written.

On Monday afternoon Sheldon found a FedEx box sitting outside his apartment door. Inside the box there was a black lunch box. Inside this, a plastic bag filled with a fine off-white powder. A short letter explained that this powder was a new antibiotic that Pierce and his benefactor had developed. It went on to state that they wanted to test it out in a large public facility like the airport. Further instructions would arrive shortly.

On Tuesday, when Sheldon arrived home from work, he found a FedEx letter leaning up against his door. Inside was a blueprint of the airport maintenance systems with an x marked by the largest of the ventilation fans in the building. The instructions were brief and to the point. At the end of your shift on Thursday go to the spot marked x on the map. Open the bag and pour the powder just inside the fan. The ventilation system will distribute the antibiotic to our subjects.

On Wednesday there was another FedEx envelope. This one contained the plane ticket to Jamaica. There was also a note stating that 100,000 dollars would be deposited into his bank account on Thursday evening after he had left work, on condition he had followed through with the task.

And now it was Thursday and he was about to make himself a new man. What's more, he might also get to be well known in the future because of the role he was playing in this research project. An antibiotic that could be administered to everyone at once -- what a breakthrough!

He knew that Pierce was not the kind of a man afraid to share the glory with others. He was certain that they would get back together again and Pierce would give him something else to do once he was back from Jamaica. Who knows? He might even meet him there.

The day passed quickly. He ate lunch in the food court with a few of the other maintenance men, celebrating the fact that he could order anything that he wanted without any concern about the price. As he sat a listened to men laugh and talk to each other, he realized that he was still a listener, sitting at the edge of life without much to say. Maybe things would be different once he got to Jamaica; once he had more money than he had ever dreamed possible to spend. In the meantime, it felt good to be sitting here with the guys, laughing out loud at the outlandish stories they were telling.

Sheldon began to feel lost when the focus of the conversation shifted to the upcoming Super Bowl. Various speakers bragged about the prowess of the team they were sure was going to win and then comparing the stats of the various quarterbacks in the league. Football wasn't something that Sheldon had paid much attention to in the past; but, as he listened to the enthusiasm of the men at the table, he wondered if it wasn't something he should look into.

The conversation veered off in a new direction when Frank, the head electrician, spoke up. "I keep hoping to be able to attend the Super Bowl in person someday, but I guess it won't be this year."

"Me too," Henry replied. "Perhaps next year when I'm retired. Has anyone ever looked into how much it would cost in all?"

A jumble of voices responded in the negative and then quieted as Tom, the newest member of their team spoke up. "My uncle went last year. He told us he spent over ten thousand dollars. I'm not sure what all that covered, but it seems like a lot to me."

"Yep, it's a lot" Frank responded. "Going to take me a few more years to save that much, just for one weekend. But oh, what a weekend that would be!"

Henry glanced at his watch and began to rise from his seat. "Time to get a move on. Got to keep on earning those dollars. Coming Sheldon?"

Sheldon also stood up and deposited his garbage in the nearest bin. Together they headed out of the food court.

As the workday drew to a close, Sheldon chose to stay in the bathroom, while the other men packed up their stuff and left the locker room. He didn't want them noticing that he wasn't rushing out the door like he usually did and he certainly didn't want to answer any questions. The room had emptied by the time he returned. He opened his locker door and removed the lunch bucket. All his years in the job meant that he didn't need the blueprint to show him the way to the ventilation fan and he quickly headed toward it. Thankfully the fan was not in an area that many people had reason to visit. He was able to reach his destination without anyone taking notice.

As he carefully poured the white powder in the assigned spot he smiled. Pierce would be so proud of him. An antibiotic that could work on everyone at once! Who would have thought? He took a deep breath as the fine powder floated upwards. He may as well make the most of it while he was here.

The next morning the plane to Jamaica left without him. Sheldon was lying in his bed at home, too weak to move and burning up with a fever like he had never felt before. He didn't even have the strength to reach for his phone to answer it when Harry called to see why he hadn't turned up for work. It took a couple of weeks before his neighbours noticed he hadn't been out of his apartment. He was dead and cold when the apartment manager finally made the effort to check on him in person.

4

FRIDAY

Jim Peterson paused at the doorway of the plane, taking a deep breath of the cold crisp air before beginning his descent down the gangway. It had been an incredibly long, tiring journey for both he and his wife Julie from the World Cattleman's Conference in Rio de Janeiro. He was so relieved to finally be home. They had traveled through four major international airports in the last three days. Rio, Atlanta, Minneapolis and Edmonton, before boarding the last plane to Grande Prairie this morning.

He smiled as his foot landed firmly on the tarmac. This was how he loved getting off a plane. Outside, in the fresh air, not hurrying through one narrow hallway after another. He was thankful that the airport in Grande Prairie had not gotten so big that it used jetways for the planes, in spite of the growth in the city that had occurred during the past few years.

His smile deepened as he remembered the indignation of a small child as his mother carried him to their seats in Minneapolis. "Mommy! You promised we would go on a plane. This is not a plane. It's just another hallway."

"I so agree with you sonny", he murmured. "It's so good to be free of the hallways."

Jim began walking towards the terminal, his long strides decreasing the distance between he and Julie, who had disembarked before him. She smiled up at him as he reached her side and took her hand in his.

"Oh Jim, she said, "thank you so much for this trip. It has been unbelievable. But I am so glad to be home again."

"So am I", he replied, "There's nothing that compares to being in the Peace River Country. I just hope that cows put off calving a few days so that I can catch up on my sleep."

"That would be nice" she responded, as they entered the building and headed towards the baggage carousel.

The next morning, Jim entered the kitchen with a puzzled look on his face. All was dark and silent. He had risen early and spent a couple of hours outdoors with the cattle and now returned to the house anticipating a full breakfast. The smell of coffee that was usually filling the air when he came in, wasn't. This was so unlike Julie.

He was about to call out her name as he removed his parka, when he remembered the long days they had just gone through. She's probably still asleep, he thought, and turned to the sink to fill the carafe for the morning's coffee. As the water began dripping down through the filter, he headed upstairs to their bedroom on tiptoes. He hoped that he wouldn't wake her if she was asleep.

She wasn't sleeping. Instead, she was staring at the door with glazed eyes as he entered the room. "Oh Jim", she whispered. "I'm so glad you are here. I don't know what is wrong with me. I am so sick. I am too weak to even get out of bed."

Jim approached the bed and rested his hand on her forward. "Darling you are burning up!"

"I know. Oh, the cold feels so good."

Jim snatched his hand back. "I'm sorry. I forgot. I have been outside."

"Oh no, it's nice, put it back, or maybe even better wet a facecloth with cold water. But first you better help me to the bathroom before I pee the bed!"

"No problem", he said with a smile, throwing back the covers, picking her up and carrying her into the ensuite with ease. "Haven't had the pleasure of doing this for few years." As he gently placed her on the toilet she began to shiver uncontrollably. He wrapped his arms around her, in an attempt to keep her warm, as the fluids gushed out from her body. A putrid smell filled the room. They both gagged as he flushed the toilet and carried her back to the bed.

"What was that?" she cried out. "I have never smelled anything so disgusting in my life. And it came from my body!"

She carefully began to pull the blankets up over her shoulders and then stopped "Jim, I think I am going to throw up."

He reacted quickly, pulling a basin from under the sink in the ensuite and handing it to her. "Here you go, darling", just as the vomit spewed out of her mouth.

"Oh Jim, I'm so sorry", she cried when the retching had finally subsided. "You have so much to do. You don't need to be looking after to me too."

"You are far more important than anything else, darling." He picked up the basin and carried it into the bathroom to empty it. As he did so, a chill raced down his spine. Bright streaks of blood were falling into the toilet along with the vomit. Jim took a deep breath, in an attempt to keep his voice as calm as possible. He turned to face the bed. "Well, I don't know what this is, but I think we had better get you to the doctor. It looks like you picked up something on the trip."

5

SATURDAY

Margret smiled as she waited for John's face to appear on the iPad in her hands. She was so glad to be living in an age when technology had arrived at the point where she and John could communicate face to face, no matter how far they were apart. It was not so long ago that they took that safari to Africa; 2006, if she remembered it correctly, when they couldn't even access their e-mail out of country. And now, only a few years later, everything was accessible from anywhere in the world. Her thoughts flew back to her childhood, listening to people predicting being able to see each other on a screen when on the telephone. Her attempts trying to conceive what this would actually look like produced nothing like a notebook or a cell phone had come to her mind back then and now it was difficult to imagine anyone living without them. This brought thoughts of her grandmother and how open she had been to accepting this world of technology. She was so glad that the girls had asked their grandmother to install WIFI in the house so they could facetime with her. It sure made things easier now, than having to depend on the land line.

"Hello darling, how are you?" John's voice filled the room as his face replaced hers on the screen.

"Oh John, it's so good to see you! We're doing well here. Been so busy that I have hardly had any time to think. So far, I've made it to the lawyer, completed the arrangements with the funeral home and have begun to go through the house to see what I want to take back to Minnesota with me. We've booked Trinity for the funeral next Saturday, so you should have plenty of time to get here."

"That's great! The big game is tomorrow. People are pouring into the city like you wouldn't believe. To be honest, it's a little too chaotic for me and I'll be glad to let Nick have this assignment back again next year. But I am glad that I'm going to experience it once. I will have to stay and wrap up some interviews after the game, but I'll be on the plane on Monday. I have changed my ticket to Grande Prairie via Edmonton and so I should be arriving on the late flight. 9 PM I think. Let's see.... here it is. Yes, 9:10 PM. This should give me lots of time to help you before the funeral. How are the girls doing? Getting bored yet?"

"Yes, I'm afraid so. They've spent some time sorting things with me, but they really aren't too interested in the past. And to be honest, the more time I spend looking at this stuff, the less interested I am in taking it back to the States with me."

"You can take anything you want. If it doesn't fit in the Dodge, we can pack it up and ship it, you know."

"Of course, but right now all I see with any value are the photo albums. Maybe my mind will have changed by the time you get here."

"And as for the girls", she continued, "thankfully they have their laptops with them, so they are able to keep up with their friends back home. They have absolutely no interest in going out and meeting anyone here. They claim it would be a waste of time considering we are returning home right after the funeral and that there will be no reason to ever come back here now that Grandma is gone. I can't say that I blame them."

"They did take their schoolwork with them, didn't they?"

"Oh yes, but it only took a few hours for them to get through that here, with what they did while we were driving and so on. Amazing to think that it was a month's worth of work in the classroom. "

Margret paused for a moment and then took a deep breath. "I'm a bit worried about Marisa. She is not talking as much as she used to. It seems that the police haven't had any luck finding out who accosted the girls before we left and that there have been reports of a couple of similar incidents at schools on the other side of the city. Those girls weren't so lucky. They haven't been seen or heard from since."

"That's terrible! I certainly hope they have this all cleared up by the time we get back home. Whoops. There's someone knocking at my door. I'll get back to you after the game tomorrow. In the meantime, give each of them a hug from me, will you and tell them I love them. Sleep well my love!"

"You too, darling."

Margret's smile faded as she turned off her iPad. She was so tired of having to be in charge. She was so tired of claiming that everything was all right. It would be so good to have John here taking over all that had to be done. She yawned as she reached over and switched off the lamp, slid down between the covers and snuggled her head into the pillows. Monday. He'd be here on Monday. Then she could hand everything over to his capable hands. She hoped she could hold things together at least that long.

6

SUNDAY

Dr. Frank Sullivan looked directly into the eyes of his best friend seated at the table across from him. "I am so sorry, Jim. We did everything that we could for Julie, but we don't know what we are dealing with. We couldn't save her." Tears filled his eyes, as he continued on, "how on earth are we going to be able to go on without her?"

Jim squeezed his eyes shut, in a desperate attempt to hold back his tears. "I don't know. I don't know. I don't know. She's been everything to me since we were children." His hands tightened around the coffee cup he was holding. "And you too. We were such a team, the three of us. Who knows – she might have married you if you hadn't gone off to medical school."

"That's a laugh, she was born a on a farm and she was a farm girl through and through. I can't imagine her living anywhere else. Yes, I loved her too, but you were the one who gave her the life she wanted."

Jim opened his eyes and gave Frank a slight smile." Yes, she was a true farmer, wasn't she? Better than me, in so many ways. Tough enough to do anything that needed doing. Oh

Frank, I so wish I hadn't taken her on that trip. Then I'd still have her with me. In the midst of that, she enjoyed it so much! You should have seen her dancing the samba. How she could move her feet that fast was beyond me. I stumbled around like a new born colt trying to keep up with her."

A nurse appeared in the cafeteria door. She called out softly, "Excuse me, Dr. Sullivan, I'm sorry, but we need you.", as she tilted her head in the direction of the emergency ward.

"I'll be right there", he responded and then turned back to Jim. "Duty calls, but you know I'm here for you, if you need me."

"Of course," Jim replied, "but don't worry about me. I'll be okay."

As Frank stood up to leave, he leaned forward and touched Jim's hand. "Jim, you're burning up! I need to admit you."

Jim pushed Frank's hand away. "I can't. You know I can't. It's calving season, and you know what that's like. I have to be there." Tears slipped down his cheeks as he also rose to leave. "I love you Frank, and I know you want to help, but if you couldn't do anything for Julie why do you think it's any different for me?"

Shoulder to shoulder, they walked out of the cafeteria together. They paused for a moment in the hallway, looking deep into each other's eyes. "I'll let you how I'm doing buddy," Jim mumbled softly and turned and walked towards the exit with his head held high.

The drive back to the farm was difficult. It was compounded by the tears that he couldn't keep in check and the foggy feeling in his brain which may have been due to grief, shock or perhaps even the reality that he had come down with the same illness that had killed his beloved wife. He knew that he shouldn't be driving in this state, but he needed to get home.

Image after image of Julie flashed through his mind as he drove. The smudge of flour that always appeared on her right cheek when she was making bread; the absolute delight in her eyes as she watched a jaguar crouched on the bank of the Pantanal River while they were in Brazil; his eyes meeting hers as she came down the aisle towards him on her father's arm; her eyes bursting with pride as she lead her 4-H steer around the ring after winning Grand Champion; and, how totally exhausted she was after the birth of their son. So many years together. So many precious memories and so many more experiences that he wanted to share with her. But she was gone. The tears began to flow again.

Frank, Julie and Jim had been a threesome since they were in diapers. Born within months of each other, their mothers had formed an impromptu baby club long before these became a trend. Of course, the proximity of their homes also played a major role in their ability to be together. Frank's dad farmed the land next Jim's and Julie's family lived across the road. Jim and Julie added her family's land to their farming operation shortly after their marriage, while her parents continued to live in the house she had grown up in. Her parents! Jim closed his eyes and shook his head trying to clear the fog that was enveloping his brain. They needed to know. This was going to be tough, but it couldn't be avoided. As he reached the driveway to the farm, he gritted his teeth and turned right instead of left.

Later that evening, Jim carefully placed the alarm clock back on the mantel after resetting it and turning it back on. Every hour on the hour. This was the reality of calving season during a Peace River winter. Once the cows starting calving, one never knew exactly how long their labour would take. With the freezing temperatures it didn't take long for a calf to die if it wasn't dried off quickly. And so, every hour Jim made that excursion back to the barn to check on the progress the herd was making. He and Julie had made the decision to push back calving a couple of weeks this year because of the trip to Brazil, which meant that the majority of the cows were coming due at the same time. It had been a good decision as there had been no births while they were on the trip and her father was looking after the herd. But it didn't take long for the first newborn to arrive, once they were back. Already there were 3 little heifers lying in the straw in the shed next to their mothers. By morning there likely would be a few more.

Jim took a deep breath as he stepped out into the cold night air. He stopped for a moment and inhaled again, this time paying attention to the scent of the wind. A chinook was on its way. A slight grin softened his face. A chinook. This was going to make things easier. He still would have to keep his eye on what was happening out in the barn, but the little ones wouldn't freeze if the temperature climbed above zero. A chinook would bring relief and he hoped the rest of the cows would make the most of this timing. One never knew how long it would last before the temperatures would plummet again.

7

MONDAY

Margret was sitting on the back step of her grandmother's house when she heard the ring of her iPhone in the kitchen. A chinook had arrived overnight and now the temperature was a balmy 5 degrees Celsius. By noon the wind had died down. The sun, shining directly on to the back step, had enticed her outside. The boys across the way had set up two hockey nets and were engaged in a noisy game of street hockey. It included shouting a loud "car" whenever a vehicle approached and the swift removal of the nets to the sidewalk. Mrs. Thompson was beating the dust out of a small rug on her porch railing next door, while Sam Shepherd was refilling the bird feeder on his front lawn. Nothing ever changes here, thought Margret, as she watched the chickadees flit amongst the branches of the shrub next to Sam's head. I likely watched this same scene as a child.

She jumped up, headed into the house and reached her phone at the same time as Marisa entered the kitchen.

"Who is it Mom?" She asked. "Dad should be on the plane now, shouldn't he?'

"Yes, but he can call from the plane." She slid her finger across the screen and said "hello".

John's voice filled her ears. "Have you been watching the news?"

"No. I've been enjoying the sunshine? Why?"

"Well, we have a problem. People are sick all over the place here. It's some kind of influenza it seems, but not one the doctors are used to. People are even dying from it. The authorities have managed to figure out that everyone who is sick went through the airport in the last couple of days so believe that's the source. Word is that it was some kind of a terrorist attack aimed at the Super Bowl. I'm lucky because I arrived a week early; but in the meantime, I can't fly out today because they've closed the airport."

"No!!" I was so looking forward to your arrival tonight. I thought you were on the plane now. "

"Believe me, I wish I was; but it looks like it will take a little longer for me to get there. I'm trying to rent a car right now and I'll drive to the next airport and see if I can get my flight out of there. In the meantime, there's a couple of things I would like you to do. Is Marisa near? I'd like her to be in on this."

Yes, she's right here. I'll switch over to speaker."

"Hi Dad."

"Hi darling. Good to hear your voice. Now, can both of your listen carefully? I don't have a good feeling on what's going on here. So, first of all, I want you to start paying close intention the local news. If you hear anything, anything at all, about an influenza outbreak in Grande Prairie, I want you to lock all the doors and stay in the house until I get there. And in order to make that possible, I want you to get in the Dodge right now and go to Costco and buy all the food that you can manage. Knowing your grandmother, she likely already has quite a bit stock piled up, but it doesn't hurt to have more. At least a month's supply or more, okay. Plus, toilet paper and water and all those other things we can't live without. I don't want us to end up having to run to the store if this flu goes rampant and I have a feeling it might."

"We can do that Dad."

"But John, how am I going to pay for it?"

"Use the credit card. Don't worry about the payment. I'll look after everything when I get there. And in the meantime, stay safe, please. Oh yes, one more thing: fill the car with gas when you go out so it's ready to leave when I get there. I think that's all." He paused for a moment and then said, "Got to go. I'm at the front of the line here. See you soon, my darlings and give Joelle a big hug from me."

The phone went silent. Marisa and Margret stood staring at each other in shock for a few minutes. It was Marisa who finally broke the silence.

"Mom, get your keys. We've got to get moving, if we are going to get all this food bought. I'll get Joelle."

That evening Margret turned on the national news for the first time since she had arrived at her grandmother's. She was expecting to see a story on the influenza outbreak at the Super Bowl; however, it was much, much bigger than that. It appeared that every city and country in the world was affected. Government officials were reporting that all of the international airports throughout the world had been contaminated in some way. Few details were being released, though the reporters were speculating that a catastrophe of epidemic proportions was eminent. People were dying. Lots of people were dying. In an attempt to stop the spread of the virus, every airport in the world had been shut down until further notice.

Margret sat staring at the screen with tears in her eyes. John had said he was driving to the next airport and now there was no next airport. She took a deep breath and let it out slowly, in an attempt to calm her racing heart. She closed her eyes to picture his face in her mind. What would he do? A few minutes passed before the answer came. He was a resourceful man. She knew that this wouldn't stop him. If he couldn't fly, he would drive.

Margret reached for her iPad and tapped on google maps. As she traced the road up to Grande Prairie she began breathing easier. That's not so bad. If he came directly north without stopping, he should be able to make it here in about 4 days. But he would likely have to sleep at some point; so, that would make it 5 or more. In that case, she was going to have to postpone the funeral.

Sleep did not come easy that night. Memories of all the airports she had travelled through filled her mind. She realized that it wasn't just the travellers and flight crews that would be affected. It would be everyone: all the sales clerks, the cooks and waiters in the restaurants, security people, cleaning crews, shoe shine boys, maintenance people and luggage handlers. She had always thought about airports as mini cities when she walked through them, places where one could have access to anything they wanted. And now, it seemed they had all become threats to the human population.

It was unbearable to fathom the reality of the situation. She closed her eyes and began reciting the alphabet. It was the only way she knew to stop thinking when her mind was this active. The boring repetition worked. She drifted off to sleep.

Vivid dreams filled her night. She was running through an airport looking for John. As she ran through the crowded concourse people ahead of her would crumple and fall to the floor, blocking her path so that she had to slow down to go around them, or carefully step over them. It was getting more and more difficult to work her way through crowd. John appeared off in the distance. She called out his name, waving the ticket she had in her hand, trying to catch his attention, but he ignored her. The people at her feet began to reach up their arms begging her to help them, but she didn't know what to do. She tried to continue on towards John, but her legs wouldn't move. He gradually disappeared in the distance as she held out her arms towards him.

She awoke the next morning to a pillow soaked with tears.

8

TUESDAY

Jim stood at the kitchen sink, staring out at the sunrise over the back pasture and tentatively raised a saltine cracker to his lips. He had been living on ginger ale ever since he had brought Julie to the hospital and had realized that he likely had the same illness as she had. The ginger ale hadn't helped much with the vomiting and diarrhea but at least it didn't taste so bad when it came out. However, he knew he would have to start eating something soon. He was getting weaker every day and there were still a lot of calves to be born. He nibbled on the corner of the cracker and wished that Julie was standing beside him witnessing this sunrise. It was absolutely gorgeous.

Yesterday had been a tough day. It started with phone calls to the children letting them know their mother had passed on. Both of them were in university this year and he knew he had to be early if he was going to catch them before classes. Both of them wanted to start for home right away but he advised then to stay put until he confirmed when the funeral was going to take place.

Between the times he spent out in the corral with the cows, he had focused on trying to make arrangements with the Bear Creek Funeral home for Julie. When he finally got through on the phone, they told him that they were swamped with the number of bodies arriving from the hospital. It seemed that every person who had flown into Grande Prairie from either Edmonton or Vancouver had come in contact with the virus and were dying. Yes, they were expecting his call. Dr. Sullivan had made the arrangements and had sent Julie's body over. They had been waiting for his call so that they could make the final arrangements to cremate her.

"Cremate her?" I haven't told you to cremate her."

"It's not a choice. The doctors are asking us to cremate everyone in order to ensure that this virus doesn't spread any further than it has. Now, I've just taken down your phone number. We'll get back to you when we have set a time for her, okay? I've got to get back to the people coming in the door."

Jim closed his eyes as he remembered that conversation. Julie was going to be cremated. What would she think of that? They had never spent any time talking over funeral details with each other. And now all those decisions had been ripped out of their hands. Suddenly, the sun burst forth on the horizon bathing the sky in gold. This is why Julie loved this window so. At least he knew what he was going to do with her ashes. He'd spread them in the pasture so that she could see that sunrise every morning.

As he thought about Julie, a memory flashed through Jim's mind: sauerkraut. If Julie was here, she'd be insisting he eat sauerkraut. She claimed that it was the fastest and most effective treatment for diarrhea, better than anything a doctor could give you. She always had sauerkraut on hand, just in case they needed it.

Jim turned to the pantry and began pushing cans aside to see if he could find any sauerkraut. Yes, here it was. He took it out and stood looking at the can in his hands for a few minutes. He had never really liked sauerkraut but if it would stop the diarrhea, he was game to try.

As he opened the can he wondered if he should heat it up. Cold or hot had never made a real difference in the taste he decided. He may as well save time and eat it cold. He dipped a fork into the can letting the juice drip into the sink in front of him before he raised it to his lips. His voice cracked a little as he said, "here's to you Julie. I don't know what this is going to do for me, but I'll either be joining you or have the energy to bring the rest of the calves into the world." Slowly and carefully he ate everything in the can, trying his best not to grimace as he did so.

A knock sounded on the back door as he was dropping the can into the recycle bin. He turned to face it, as it opened. His father-in-law appeared in the doorway.

"Hey, Jim. How's it going?"

"Pretty good, we've got 25 calves already so there's still more to go. All healthy. This warm weather has certainly helped a lot."

"Have you had any time to watch the news?"

"No", Jim chuckled." That's the last thing on my mind."

"Well, there's some guy on there claiming that he has a vaccination for whatever Julie had. Claiming that that he had got wind of this virus being created in a lab back in

2008 or thereabouts and that he was worried that some terrorists might get their hands on it so he started working on developing a vaccination, just in case. Says he's got enough stockpiled for most of the world and is making more. Claims he is willing to sell the vaccines to any government that is willing to buy them - for millions of course! As far as I understand, they're lining up fast to get it.

"Wow, who'd have thought? He started planning all this way back in 2008. That's remarkable. But then this whole situation is like something out of a movie isn't it?"

"Yeah, that's what Mary and I were just saying this morning. It's like a plot in a movie that we've somehow got ourselves mixed up in. Anyway, they are advising people to keep their eyes on the news because there will be announcements coming as to when the vaccines are available. Mary wants to be first in line. We'll pick you up if you want.

"No, that's okay. Thanks for the info and let me know when they are available. I'll pop in to the city between calves."

I won't be taking any vaccination, thought Jim, as he watched Peter drive away. He didn't want to let him know that he was already sick. They didn't need to worry any more than they already were. And who knows? He was still alive which is more than one could say about anyone else who had been in the airports. Maybe he would survive. If so, his immune system would be able to take care of him. But in the meantime, he had better let the kids know about this. He didn't want to lose them too.

The shrill ring of the alarm clock filled the air as he hung up the phone. "Here we go again," he murmured as he reached over to shut it off and adjust the time to the next hour. He pulled on his boots and parka and headed back to the barnyard.

9

WEDNESDAY

It was the voice that caught Margret's attention as she entered the living room -- deep, passionate, mesmerizing. Margret closed her eyes for a moment, letting the sound wash over her. It was like swimming in honey.

Marisa and Joelle were so engrossed in what was happening on the screen, they were oblivious to her presence. She watched them for a few minutes, overcome by their beauty and the love she had for them. Then she approached the set, trying to make out what had captivated their attention to this degree. A reporter was pointing the microphone towards a rather nondescript man, from whom this incredible voice was emanating. Margret frowned, trying to place either of them in her memory, but there was nothing there. She was good with faces. Obviously, she hadn't seen either of them before. The man who was talking had dark hair, dark eyes and was of medium height and build. There was nothing remarkable about him, except for that voice, what a voice! One didn't want it to stop.

As the program broke for a commercial Joelle turned to her mother and cried out. "Mom, Mom there's hope! There's a vaccine. This man has developed a vaccine for the flu everyone is getting. The terrorists are not going to win."

"What do you mean? A vaccine for what is killing the people at the Super Bowl?"

"Killing people all over the world, Mom."

"This man claims he has a cure?"

"He isn't saying it's a cure," Marisa interjected." He's saying that if we take the vaccination we won't be affected by the virus."

"We'll be safe. Isn't that exciting?" Joelle could hardly contain herself as she beamed up at her mother.

"Come, sit down and listen. He's been telling the whole story and it's quite a story. His parents died when he was very young and he was taken in by a scientist who worked in the pharmaceutical industry creating medicines. He spent a lot of time in the lab with his benefactor while he was growing up and got interested in viruses. Anyway, when he heard that someone had created this virus in a lab, a virus that could possibly wipe out the whole population of the world back in 2008, he got worried that some terrorist organization might get their hands on it. He has been working on a vaccine for it ever since. He just finished describing how he had befriended this man and convinced him that he wanted him for his mentor so that he could gain access to the virus."

"Ssssh! It's back on again."

All three women turned their attention back to the television screen. The focus of the program moved into a laboratory where the scientist claimed to have created the vaccine. Heartbreaking videos of monkeys being subjected to the virus filled the screen, complete with a warning that these scenes may be disturbing to some viewers. They were followed by graphic scenes of their agonizing deaths. Other monkeys were vaccinated before they were exposed to the virus. They all survived and appeared healthy. The reporter asked if he could see the actual virus but was denied with claims that it would be far too dangerous to expose him. Finally, shots of a warehouse appeared. Millions of vials of the vaccine waited to be deployed around the world. The speaker claimed he would release them to each country once their government had paid for them.

The voice resonated throughout the report, sharing these details with the world. A voice so calm, so controlled and so convincing, its listeners were almost hypnotized. And then suddenly, it was gone. The screen went black. Silence filled the room. Both girls turned to stare at their mother. All three gasped for air at the same time, as they realized that they had all been holding their breath.

After a moment of hollow silence, the reporter spoke again. "You have been listening to an interview with the saviour of mankind and soon to become the richest man in the world -- Pierce Paxton."

10

THURSDAY

Frank slumped in his chair at the conference table, trying desperately to keep his eyes open. He couldn't remember when he had last slept. The stress of the last five days was beyond anything he had ever imagined. Fighting desperately to save Julie's life, only to lose her, was devastating. The situation had gone from bad to worse since then as the people kept pouring into the emergency room. They were searching for help, but all had died within 48 hours, no matter what the staff did. The medical staff hadn't managed to save anyone: oil patch workers flying in from the east coast; grandparents here to welcome their new grandchild into the family; newly married couples returning from their Caribbean honeymoon; and, worst of all, whole families who had just returned from their dream trip to Disneyland. The list went on and on. Frank had lost count of how many he had tried to help, and he was only one of the doctors on staff. There were hundreds of casualties whose only fault had been relying on the airlines to get them where they wanted to go.

Frank knew it wasn't over. Closing the airports was a major step in eliminating the direct contact the virus, but the next wave of casualties was about to arrive: those who been in direct contact with those who were ill. Several of the nurses were already taking up beds in the hospital, fighting for their own lives. He would likely have to join them soon. He snapped his head sideways trying to clear the fog from his brain and gulped down the coffee someone had just set in front of him. Lucy, the head nurse in the hospital, who was sitting directly across from him, caught his eye and raised her cup towards him. She looked as exhausted as he was.

But there was hope. Hope in the form of a vaccine and that was why they were all concentrated in this room, rather than working with their patients. People from every organization that had anything to do with health in the region were present, occupying not only the chairs around the conference table, but also all the extra chairs that had been brought in. Others were standing leaning against the walls. As Frank glanced around the room, he recognized faces from all over: the hospital in Beaverlodge, the college nursing program, the health unit, the pulp mill, nursing homes, as well as the fire hall and police station. There were even a couple of dentists in the room. It appeared that whoever had pulled this group together had thought of everyone.

The face of the provincial health minister filled the screen at the far end of the room. She began by thanking everyone present for their diligence and cooperation, in the midst of the worst medical disaster to ever hit the province. She was pleased to announce that the federal government had made arrangements to purchase and to deliver enough vaccines for every citizen in Canada. The vaccines were already in the air on their way to Canada and would be distributed throughout the country by Federal Express as swiftly as possible.

She went on to explain that she had called all of the groups throughout the province together so that they could work out a specific plans for their areas, to vaccinate as many people as quickly as possible. She closed her presentation with these words: "this is a time for action. I don't want to waste your time talking. I will close now so that you can get to work organizing the largest and fastest mass vaccination program in the history of our province. I trust you will do a good job. God be with you." Her face faded from the screen as a list of cities appeared with the anticipated time of arrival of the vaccine for each one.

Chaos ensued as everyone in the room began to offer different suggestions that they felt important. The fire chief stepped forward and called for order. The head of the health unit jumped up, prepared to write a list of suggestions on the white board. Someone suggested dividing the list into categories: who would vaccinate, where the vaccinations would take place and how the vaccines would be delivered. Another person suggested involving the radio and television stations. Three more people rose and took their places at the white board.

The doctor from Beaverlodge suggested that it might be better to take the vaccines out to the rural communities rather than have all the people drive into the city. The director of Stars said they could deliver the vaccines to rural communities, as long as there was someone prepared to do the vaccinations. Someone else suggested checking the latest census to determine where people lived so that a proper number of vaccines would be available.

Frank put up his hand. When the fire chief pointed at him, he volunteered to continue looking after the hospital. He also said he would cut his staff to the minimum to look after the current patients. This would allow those who were not at the hospital to help with the vaccinations.

Lucy also put up her hand. "We can use anyone who is trained in using needles to help vaccinate. I'll start pulling a list together if you want."

Someone suggested using the hallways in the two malls as distribution points. There'd be lots of room to set up as well as parking space for everyone coming in. What's more, the buses go to the malls for those who don't drive.

"There's a lot of churches with big halls. They also have parking lots."

Another voice chimed in, "What about the schools?" Should we keep the schools open and have teams go into each of them? "

Everyone stopped for a second and looked at one another. "I don't think so," said one of the school nurses. "I think that parents are going to want to be with their children through this. What about closing the schools and using them as a distribution point? That will open up more space."

"The schools would likely be the best spot in the rural communities, but I think the malls are a better choice here in Grande Prairie."

Frank was getting dizzy. The room was getting warmer by the minute and the coffee he had ingested was beginning to feel very uncomfortable in his stomach. He put up his hand again and asked if he could excuse himself. "I'll leave this in your very capable hands," he said and reminded everyone that he would look after the hospital. Lucy rose and followed him out of the room saying," I'll get to work on a list of people who can help us vaccinate."

Lucy caught up to Frank just as he left the building. "Are you okay?" she asked.

"No," he replied. "I'm afraid not. I've got it too. That's why I volunteered to stay at the hospital. May as well not expose others needlessly."

Lucy caught his hand and squeezed it tightly. "Me too. Put me on your list of necessary staff once I'm done putting this list together."

11

FRIDAY

The sun had just begun to peak over the horizon when Margret stumbled down the stairs and into the living room. She automatically switched on the television as she went by it and headed into the kitchen to make coffee. It was funny how little attention she had paid to television in the last few years. And, how now, since John told her about the virus, she had to have it on all the time.

A familiar face filled the screen. "Richard Parvinski. You haven't changed a bit!" muttered Margret as she sat down, waiting for the coffee to perk. Richard was standing in front of the main doors of the Prairie Mall, urging everyone listening to come down and get their vaccination as soon as possible.

The reporter retrieved the microphone and said "Thank you Mayor Parvinski, this is what true leadership is about: stepping forward in a time of a crisis situation."

"Being a leader, my ass," muttered Margret. "I doubt it. Just protecting your own interests and using your position to get your family in line, first."

"How come you're talking to the television, Mom? Oooh, what an arrogant looking man."

"You've pegged him right, Marisa."

"You know him?"

"Yes, of course I know him. I went to school with him for eight years. He was a creep back then and it doesn't appear that the years have improved him in the slightest. Believe it or not, he's the mayor of this fine city."

"Good thing we're not planning to stay here."

"That's for sure. He's one of the reasons I'd never want to live here again. If people are dumb enough to vote for someone like him, I don't want anything to do with them."

"Well, at least he's getting his vaccination. Are we going to go and get ours today?"

"No, they want to vaccinate everyone, so it's going to take a while. Dad told us to stay in the house until he gets here. We'll be safe here until he comes and then we can all go together."

"That works for me. Well, I think I'll go upstairs and check how things are going in Minneapolis. Teri should be up and around by now."

Margret was just about to get herself a cup of coffee when the doorbell rang. "John!" she exclaimed and hurried to the door. She was about to cry out his name again as she flung the door open, when she realized that it wasn't him. It was the mailman, or in this case, one should say mailwoman, who was holding a large box.

"Parcel for Martha Crawford, I need a signature."

"I'm sorry, but she isn't here. She died."

"Oh, I'm so sorry. I guess she ordered this before she passed. It doesn't say she has to be the one to sign. You can do it for her." She looked up into Margret's face, holding a pen out expectantly. "Margret? Is that you, Margret?"

Margret studied the face of the woman before her for a few seconds. "Katie. Katie Owens! It's been years."

"Oh, my goodness! What are you doing here, especially right now with everything that's going on.?"

"Well Grandma died, and so I came up to arrange the funeral and decide what to do with the house and everything that's in it. I'm the sole beneficiary you see. And then they closed the airports so my husband couldn't get here. So, I postponed the funeral, and now we are waiting for him arrive so that we can finish up with Grandma and then go back home."

"We? Who's we?"

"My daughters and I: Marisa and Joelle. They drove up with me. Is there any chance that you have time for a cup of coffee? I just brewed a pot and it's so nice to see a familiar face."

Katie pulled out her cell phone and glanced at the screen. "Just after eight. A quick one, I guess. I got out early this morning so that I can get to the mall for my vaccination when I'm done work. Are you planning to go today?"

"No, we're waiting for John. He's driving and should be here anytime. Come on and make yourself comfortable while I get the coffee. Cream and sugar?"

"No, neither. I like it strong and black."

"Just like my men!" replied Margret and they both burst out laughing as they remembered the line that was so popular when they were in high school.

The next fifteen minutes passed very quickly as the women filled each other in on what they had been doing after they graduated. Katie said she had taken off a year to travel. Europe was incredible! She started college when she got back to Grande Prairie, but barely managed to get through one semester before she realized that studying was not what she wanted to do with her life. Then she got a job at Tim Horton's and Bruce Likeness was one of the regulars.

"Do you remember him? He was three years ahead of us at school. A quiet guy so you might not. Anyway, we got married and had three kids; two boys and a girl. I was a stay-at-home mom until Jeffrey went to grade one. I got pretty restless after that. At Christmas, the post office was hiring extra staff. Been with them ever since. And what about you?"

"Well John and I are living in Minneapolis. He's a sports reporter and had to go to the Super Bowl the day my grand-mother died. What with this virus, the airports are closed and so he's driving up here."

Marisa and Joelle interrupted their mother's story as they entered the room, lured in by the sound of two voices. Introductions followed and the girls assured the visitor that they couldn't wait to get back to the States.

Katie checked the time on her cell phone again. "Well, it looks like I had better run. This has been nice. Maybe we can have you over for supper before you leave and you can meet my family."

"That would be fun. But after John arrives, okay? We're staying put until he gets here so that we can get vaccinated together. I'd love for you meet him too."

Margret stood on the front step for a long time after Katie had disappeared down the street. The sun was shining. The sky was so blue. "Hurry up John," she murmured. "I need you."

A strange noise filled the air. Margret turned and looked south to see what was coming down the street. It was the Shriner's van, with a voice blaring through the megaphone advising everyone to get to the Prairie Mall to be vaccinated.

"Yes sir," Margret responded as she stepped back inside and closed the door, "as soon as John arrives."

12

WEDNESDAY

Jim was sound asleep on the sofa in the living room when the alarm clock rang again. His head jerked upwards and then dropped down onto the pillow. He slowly opened his eyes, yawned and struggled into a sitting position. Calving season was almost complete. There were ninety-five beautiful pure-bred Simmental calves out in the barnyard now, almost doubling the size of the herd. Julie would be so pleased. But he couldn't stop yet. There were still five more to go. He struggled to his feet and headed into the kitchen. Coffee, I need coffee. He stopped short! This was the first time his body had wanted anything since that last morning with Julie. Yes, he drank a lot of ginger ale and forced himself to eat the sauerkraut; but he hadn't had any actual desire for nutrients of any kind in days. This was amazing. He smiled as he walked into the kitchen and turned on the tap to fill the coffee pot.

A couple of hours later, Jim was back in the kitchen looking for food. Another calf had arrived while he was sleeping, but the warmer temperatures meant that she wasn't in danger of freezing. However, one of the cows was not doing well and Jim realized that he would have to pull this calf. He slipped a halter over the cow's head and tied her securely to the corral. He so wished that Julie was here to help. She was so calm in times like this and the animals reacted so well to her. He pulled on the long sterile gloves and reached deep into the womb to see if he could feel what was obstructing the birth process. Yes, there it was. One of the back feet was caught on the hip bone. He straightened it out and stood back for a while, waiting to see if this would help. Nothing happened. The cow obviously was exhausted and had no energy left to push.

His arm went back into the womb, this time with a small noose on the end of a rope. He slipped the noose around both of the back feet, tightened it, stepped back and slowly and gently began to pull. It was a success and Jim smiled as the calf slid out onto the ground behind its mother. He took the noose off its feet and then untied the cow's halter and removed it from her head. She immediately turned and began sniffing her baby. Once she determined it was okay, she began the process of washing it. As her long tongue swept over the body of the calf, Jim stepped back to let nature take its course. He was relieved. This calf was going to be okay. So often they weren't when he had to pull them.

The fridge was basically empty with only a few condiments stored the door. "Shoot" muttered Jim. No wonder -- I haven't been shopping since we got back. Julie had done a great job of clearing out everything that might spoil before they left for Brazil. He turned to the pantry to see what he could find. Nothing there looked very appetizing either. "What I want is a full breakfast of bacon and eggs" he muttered. He picked up his phone and said "call Mary." It began to ring. When she answered he asked "Any chance you can feed me? I'm looking for some bacon and eggs and there's nothing in this house."

"Of course, dear. That's no problem. Come on over. I'll get right on it."

Jim slipped on his coat, grabbed his keys and headed out the door to his pickup. It would be good to spend some time with his in-laws.

Later that afternoon, Jim returned to the house. He was so glad that he had been able to avoid talking about Julie while he was eating. Peter and Mary were so full of details of what was happening in Grande Prairie with the vaccinations that there wasn't any time for anything else. They had gone to the Prairie Mall because it sounded like it was the biggest distribution point.

"I expected chaos," said Peter, "considering what's at stake, but it was all quite orderly. You got a number at the door and found the table that matched your number, waited in line for a few minutes, got your shot and that was it. There were a lot of tables; a lot, lining each side of the hall with doctors or nurses at each of them."

"They weren't all doctors and nurses," interjected Mary. "Mine was just a mother of a diabetic child. It looked like they had everyone in the city who knew how to do an injection there. I saw one of the firemen at one table and my dentist at another."

"Do you know what it reminded me of? The fire in Fort McMurray a few years back. All those people driving through the flames and not one of them trying something crazy and causing an accident. Maybe we react differently when our lives are on the line."

"Anyway, we're safe now," said Mary. "I only wish that Julie would have had this chance." Tears filled her eyes. Jim reached for her hand and squeezed it.

"You make sure you get in there Jim," she continued. "I know you put the cattle before everything, especially at this time of the year, but we can't afford to lose you too. Promise me, you'll go."

"I promise. But first I'd better get to the store and stock up on some groceries, and then back to my precious herd. I Iove you Mary, and you too, Peter. I'm so glad you'll be okay. Thanks for breakfast!"

Jim set the sacks of groceries on the counter and turned on the small television that Julie watched while she was cooking. As he unpacked the bags, he listened to different reports on the mass vaccination process. It appeared that all of the world governments had agreed to Paxton's terms and bought the vaccines. People were lining up for the shots throughout the whole world.

Jim had no intention of getting vaccinated, in spite of his promise to Mary. He knew that he had been fighting the virus; and, he knew he had succeeded, though he wasn't sure how. Perhaps it had something to do with the fact he had never had a real sleep since he got off the plane. Whatever it was, it had worked. The brain fog was gone. His stomach was no longer rolling. Yes, he was still tired, but in the midst of the exhaustion, he felt great.

As he thought about the possibilities, his mind turned to the promise he had given Frank to stay in touch. He picked up his phone and called him hoping that he wouldn't have to leave a message. However, Frank's voice, tired and weak came on after a couple of rings.

"You don't sound so good buddy."

"No, I'm not. I've got it too, but I but I volunteered to take care of the hospital while the vaccinations were being given out. So, I won't have any time for myself until Tuesday or Wednesday. How are you doing?"

"Great, actually. That's why I phoned. I've come through it. No more vomiting or diarrhea. The fog has lifted from my brain and I actually feel hungry again. I don't know why, but it appears I managed to fight it off."

"Wow! So, what did you do? We haven't come up with anything here that has helped."

"Well, I drank ginger ale and forced myself to eat a couple of cans of sauerkraut, but I don't think that is it. I haven't lain down and had a decent sleep since we got back from Brazil, what with the calving and all. Maybe the virus needs you to relax in order to take over your body completely. I might be wrong, but I have a feeling that's it."

"If that's the answer, I'm the perfect candidate to try it out on right now. Thanks for calling and good luck with the calves."

"Just one to go and then I can sleep. You take care of yourself now, hear?"

As Jim turned off the phone and headed back out to the herd, Frank was already making his way down the hospital hallway. As he entered a room, he switched on the lights and began to call out. "Judy, Lucy, wake up! I've got something to tell you!"

He gently shook the shoulder of the woman nearest the door until she opened her eyes and then moved on to the other by the window. "Listen. Jim was in four of the airports where the virus was spread. He came down with the influenza like everyone else did, but he has survived. It appears that it has something to do with staying awake as well as drinking ginger ale and eating sauerkraut. Come on, get up! We have to keep everyone awake. It appears that this is the only way we can stay alive."

13

FRIDAY

The silence hung over the room like a curse. Margret sat facing the television set, clicking the remote to change the channels, one after another. The same message appeared on each of them. This station is experiencing technical difficulties and will be off the air until future notice. She didn't know why she felt so uncomfortable. After all, television had not played a big role in her life up until last week when John had told her about the virus. Since then, it had been on almost twenty-four hours a day as she tried to keep up with what was happening in the outside world. And now she missed it. Sighing, she dropped the remote on the side table and got to her feet. Perhaps she could get the radio to work. She walked into the kitchen and turned it on, but she had the same response. No matter how slowly and carefully she moved the dial around, she couldn't find a station that was broadcasting.

The wind began to howl around the corners of the house. "Typical Alberta weather," Margret muttered. After the chinook last week, the temperature dropped; and rain, followed by snow, had started to fall. And now the wind!

Margret shook her head, thinking of how this wind would blow the newly fallen snow into hard drifts that were almost impossible to get through. No wonder it was taking John so long to get here. All of the weather gods were working against him.

"Mom", Marisa called out as she clattered down the stairs. "I can't get a hold of any of the girls back home. I've been texting them for the last hour and there's no response. This isn't like them. Do you have any idea what's going on?"

"No, I don't. The television is on the blink and I just tried the radio and there's nothing there either. Perhaps the snow has knocked out the lines or something."

"I don't think cell phones depend on lines, do they? It's more about towers and satellites than lines."

But it's a cable company that put the Wi-Fi in the house for grandma. I'm sure they have lines of some sort.

"Yeah, I suppose so, but then wouldn't my phone be giving me a message that it wasn't working? No, I'm sure there must be something going on in Minneapolis. It can't be the flu because all of them got the shot. Oh, I wish we hadn't left. I don't like being here all by ourselves. Have you heard anything from Dad yet? You said he'd be here on Tuesday at the latest and now it's already Friday!"

"No, I haven't Marisa. I expect all the snow is slowing him down. And now the wind is blowing. It's only going to make things worse."

"Have you tried to phone him, or even text him?"

"Of course I have." She didn't want to admit how many messages she had left over the past few days, to the point that his mailbox was full and she couldn't leave any more.

She didn't want Marisa to know how desperate she was beginning to feel. "He likely has turned the phone off while he's driving. You know how much he hates people using the phone while they are on the road. He'll get to us when he gets to us."

A cold chill ran down Margret's spine as she uttered those words. She couldn't understand why John wasn't calling and letting them know what was going on. It felt like he had disappeared off the face of the earth. This silence wasn't like him. Maybe the virus killed him. Maybe he was in a car accident, lying somewhere in a hospital in a coma. Maybe a bunch of vagrants had jumped him, stealing the rental car and his phone, and leaving him to die in an alley. She squeezed her eyes shut and shook her head trying to make these thoughts go away. They weren't helping at all. "I'm sure that all of his energy is focused on getting to us, Marisa. He'll be here shortly I'm sure. He is a resourceful man. "

She decided to change the subject. "Do you know what? I haven't heard the Shriner's van for a day or so. Have you?"

"No. I haven't? Maybe we have gotten so used to it we don't even hear it when it goes by."

Margret went and opened the door to look down the street but shut it again quickly, as a cold gust of wind swept into the room. Come to think of it, she hadn't heard the van with its loud message today, but she hadn't heard any other traffic either. Maybe that was why the silence felt so disturbing. No one was moving. Oh well, it was far too cold right now to investigate this situation any further.

As she surveyed the room before her, her grandmother's stereo caught her eye. Her grandfather had bought it for her shortly after they were married and she refused to replace it, no matter how many times Margret had grumbled about her not keeping up with the times. She opened it up, pulled a number of LPs from their jackets and stacked them above the turntable. She flicked the switch and the LP on the bottom of the pile dropped down. The arm with the needle swung into place. Dean Martin's rich voice filled the room, "Everybody Loves Somebody Sometime."

"Oh mother! No!" the girls voices rang out with protest from upstairs.

"It's all we got and I need something to fill in the void." Margret headed into the kitchen. She may as well get busy and make something for lunch: something special, something complicated, that would take her mind off what was happening, or perhaps she should say, not happening.

14

Jim opened his eyes and looked into the grey light of dawn. This was his favourite time of the day. There was a soft stillness which held the promise of new things to come. He swung his legs out of the bed and padded through the familiar rooms of the house without the need of lights. When he reached the kitchen, he stopped at the sink and looked out over the pasture. Pastel colours were just beginning to fill the sky. In no time the sun would burst over the horizon, filling this room with light. In the meantime, he chose to make the most of the dawn.

He reached over to pick up the coffee pot and turned on the tap to fill it. Nothing happened. He frowned and turned the tap off and then on again. Again, nothing happened. "Something must be wrong with the pump" he muttered and headed towards the basement to check it out. He reached out to switch on the light as he began his descent down the stairs. Nothing happened. Oh, the electricity must be off. Bummer. Now what am I going to do about coffee?

He was standing in front of the fireplace in the living room when Frank stumbled down the stairs, his hair tousled and his eyes half open. "Coffee, I need coffee," he cried out. He gave Jim a puzzled look and asked "What are you doing in here?"

"Well I'm trying to decide how to make you coffee. Is it better to light a fire here and cook it or out on the barbecue on the patio? I'm thinking it's better here, as it won't be as cold as it is on the patio, but it has been so long since I made a fire in this thing, I don't know if I remember how. Julie was so good at it."

"Why don't you just make it the usual way?"

"What, the fire?"

"No, the coffee."

"I can't". No electricity."

"The electricity is off? Well that's a bummer? Just the house, or what?"

"Not sure. Lights aren't working, and there's no water so the pump isn't working either. I expect we don't have a furnace either as it needs electricity to turn it on as well as run the fan. But I thought I would make the coffee before I did anything else. I know how addicted you are to it."

"Oh yeah, I believe that. It's only me you're thinking about." Frank chuckled. "You're twice as addicted as me. So, what do you think? Do you want to get dressed and drive in to Tim Horton's and pick some up, or do you want to play boy scout here with this fire? I'm buying."

Jim studied Frank's face for a few seconds and then responded, "Tim Horton's it is." Frank headed back to his bedroom to get dressed while Jim found the truck keys and pushed the remote starter button.

Frank had moved out to live with Jim on the Monday of the mass vaccinations. It wasn't that he didn't want to continue being a doctor. It was that they didn't want him anymore. Judy had gone directly to the head administrator the morning after he had awakened her with the suggestion that they needed to stay awake to fight the virus, as well as drinking ginger ale and eating sauerkraut. Marjorie Williams had called him into the office immediately and demanded to know what he was thinking. Keeping sick people awake was the last thing that would happen in a hospital that she was in charge of. It went against everything that the medical system had been based on for centuries. Everyone knew that one of the best things to heal a body was sleep. And suggesting ginger ale and sauerkraut based on some old wives' tales? He was to cease any action of this sort immediately. As Frank strode out of her office with his head high, he shed his role of a traditional doctor. It obviously wasn't working.

Frank spent most of that Sunday trying to convince people to listen to him. He talked to his patients, sharing how this system had brought Jim through the illness. He talked to all the nurses; those who were working and those who were now occupying beds in the hospital. He talked the orderlies, the security guards, the ambulance drivers and the staff in the kitchen. He even talked to the few people who were brave enough to come through the hospital doors to visit their family members. In time, word of what he was doing got back to the administrator. She summoned him back to her office again.

"I warned you, Doctor Sullivan. I told you not to spread these lies about staying awake. You're out of here. I want you to leave right away and not come back. You are banned from coming through these doors again until this crisis is over."

Frank had called Jim the next morning asking him to come and get him. Keeping himself awake at home, where he was all alone with nothing to do, had proven far more difficult than he had anticipated. He knew that he needed someone to work with him, as well as provide tasks that would keep him occupied. Jim was the only person he knew who would understand.

And so, Jim drove into town and picked him up. They stopped at the grocery store on their way out of town and bought enough food and drinks to restock the kitchen. They returned to the farm where, hour after hour, Jim made sure that Frank was awake and busy. It had taken five days in total, but he finally woke up one morning feeling like himself again. Once they knew he was clear of the virus, they both went to bed and caught up on all the sleep they had missed. Calving was complete. Together they rebuilt their run-down bodies and kept up with all the farm chores.

In the midst of this, Jim had made another run into the city to see how the mass vaccination program was going. Radio reports had indicated that it was very successful with thousands of people being vaccinated in each twenty-four-hour period. It was late Monday afternoon when he stopped at the mall. The parking lot was still full. People were coming and going. Everything looked like it was on track. However, it was a ruse. The health professionals who were administering the vaccinations were in trouble. They had all received their injections early on Friday morning and now, one by one, they were succumbing to the virus.

A chill ran down Jim's spine as he realized what was happening. He dashed out of the mall and ran to his truck, driving back to the farm as fast as he could. When he reached the driveway, he turned right again, instead of left.

He found both Peter and Mary lying together in their bed with basins of blood streaked vomit on the floor beside them. He franticly urged them to get up. He admitted that he had been sick too, and that he had managed to fight it off quite by accident, because he had to stay awake for the calves. They didn't have to die. They could live if they just got up and stayed up.

Peter reached over and took Mary's hand. They both shook their heads in unison, looking at Jim with tears in their eyes. It wasn't worth it. They knew they were dying, but it was okay. They were old and they were tired. Even more so, they didn't know if they wanted to live without Julie. "Just let us be, Jim. We have been so happy here. Let us die together in our own bed."

Jim reached out his hand to steady himself on the bed post as the reality of his situation hit full force. Tears began to run down his face and his body swayed in grief. Both of his children had phoned on Saturday to assure him that they had followed his instructions and been vaccinated. Neither of them had answered their phones when he had called this morning. Sobs shook his whole body as he realized they were likely too sick to call. He had lost them too. He was all alone. He wiped his eyes and forced himself to look at Mary and Peter. They didn't have to know. His voice was husky as he said, "I am going to miss you both so much. Give my darling a hug for me," before he stumbled towards the bedroom door.

"And Jim." Mary's voice was steady, though weak. "Please take care of my chickens."

He turned back and smiled at her. "Yes ma'am! You can count on that!"

And now, Jim sat in the truck, looking at the driveway in front of him. It had been weeks since he last driven on it. Between the amount of snow that had fallen and then the drifting, it was difficult to see for certain where the ditches were. He shifted the truck into four-wheel drive. This might not be the best idea, but he was pretty sure they would be able to get through to the highway and then it would be clear sailing. He stepped on the gas and off they went.

When they reached the highway, they looked at each other with concern. It looked as bad as the driveway had. Not only hadn't it been plowed, but there weren't any other vehicle tracks to be seen.

"Should we try it?" he asked Frank.

"Yep, we can do it,' replied Frank. "It will be good to know what is going on in town, as well as getting coffee."

They turned east and headed towards the city, often plowing through drifts that were above the front bumper of the truck.

"I'm sure glad I have four-wheel drive. I don't think we'd make it through this otherwise."

"Kind of an adventure, isn't it? Remember that storm of 1991 when we were on the ski trip and all the highways were closed? That was worse than this."

The first set of traffic lights wasn't working when they reached the city; a sign that the electricity outage extended much further than the farm. They turned into Tim Horton's parking lot. It was empty and covered with as much snow as the highway had been. As Jim pulled the truck up in to the front entrance, which was blocked by a huge drift, he turned to look at Frank.

"There's no one here." It was hard to speak with the lump that was forming in his throat.

Frank nodded slowly.

"There's no one here." Jim swept his hand up past the windshield, indicating all of the businesses that surrounded Tim Hortons. "No one at all. My God, what have we done? What have we done?"

"Well, not exactly we..." Frank's words died out as Jim interjected with a loud.

"NO!!, Not we, like in you and me. Of course not! We, as in mankind. This is a city of seventy thousand people and there is no one here. No one! Where are they?"

Frank bowed his head as he whispered "with Julie?"

"Yes, with Julie." Jim beat on the steering wheel with both fists as tears ran down his cheeks for several minutes. Then he wiped his eyes with his sleeve and reached down to slip the truck into reverse. As he pulled up to the highway and turned back towards the farm, he took a deep breath. "I guess it's time to start looking at our world differently. It looks like everything we have been used to taking for granted is gone. And we are going to have to learn to live without it whether we want to or not."

15

Margret sighed softly as she stood at the window looking out at the park across the street. The falling snowflakes obscured her view, painting everything in her line of vision white. Here it was, the first day of spring and the snow was still falling. Margret remembered dealing with the cold winters of northern Alberta as a child, but never had she experienced a March quite like this. February had been bad with all the snow and the wind, but March had even been worse. First the temperature had fallen close to minus 40 for a week and half and then the snow began to fall. It was still falling. Not quite what she expected for the first day of spring.

She turned and looked at her two daughters quietly reading on the sofa. Thank goodness Grandma had built up quite a library while she was alive. The books and the collection of board games had kept them sane as the days passed waiting for John to arrive. Of course, at this point, one could only read during the daylight since the electricity had gone off, but at least it gave them something to do. She turned back to the window and sighed again as the wind swept another mass of snow across the front yard.

Suddenly a picture of Natalie's face swept through her mind. Natalie, her face all covered with snow, laughing as she faced directly into the wind. Storm, they called it. Storm, the game they had made up when they were eleven, just for days like this when they would go to the park across the street to brave the elements as they set off to rescue someone, somewhere, who was in dire need. Their goals were as vast and varied as their imaginations could make them.

She turned back to the girls and said, "I'm going outside – do you want to come with me?"

"Are you crazy Mom? Look at it – it's a storm. No one goes out in a storm."

"It will be fun! I used to do it all the time when I was little."

Both girls looked at her as if she was crazy, shaking their heads in amusement as they turned back to the books they were reading. Margret refocussed her attention on the window, watching the snow dance across the street. Could she do it alone? She straightened her shoulders and smiled. Yes, she could. It wouldn't be quite as much fun, but it would definitely be a break from staying inside. She went to the closet to find the gear she would need to stay warm.

Margret took a deep breath as she stepped out on the front step. As the cold hit her lungs, she remembered how Grandma had always believed that it was the best cure for a cold. If she came home from school with even a sniffle she knew she would face a long walk with Grandma. "Breathe deep," she would remind her as they briskly walked along, side by side. "Breathe deep. An hour breathing deep out in the cold will kill any germs wanting to make a home in your body". And Margret had to admit it was a good remedy. The two of them were rarely sick.

Bracing herself against the wind, Margret started down the sidewalk towards the park. Then she paused for a moment considering the possibilities. She was too old to play Storm any more, but now that she was outside, she wasn't going to give up this opportunity to see how the community was faring. She turned away from the park and headed down the street in the opposite direction. She was relieved to discover that walking proved to be easier than she remembered from the past. Of course, her legs were longer now than when she was a child, but the ease had far more to do with the fact the drifting snow had packed itself solid and she was able to walk on top of it.

With the wind howling around the corners of the houses, it took Margret a few minutes to notice how silent the rest of the world was. It also looked untouched. The sidewalks and road were covered in snow in much the same way as the lawns that bordered them. She glanced at each of the houses as she passed. They were dark and silent with snowdrifts blown up against their doorways. No smoke rose from the chimneys. No lights appeared in any of the windows. A sudden feeling of foreboding swept over her. She was all alone in the world. She glanced back to see the smoke rising from their fireplace chimney and smiled. She knew there were others waiting for her there. She was okay.

When she reached the end of the street, she glanced to the left and the right, trying to decide which way to go. The road was still untouched by human traffic. The world was still silent. As she looked left, she saw the corner grocery store about a half a block away. Mr. and Mrs. White had owned and operated that store for as long as she could remember. She started toward it, all the while calculating how old they would be now. They were newly married when she had arrived at her grandmother's at age ten. She was now 43. That meant they would be in their mid-fifties, too early for retirement. She hastened her steps towards the store. It would be so good to see them again.

When she arrived, she realized that the store was as dark and deserted as the houses she had passed had been. The large window which displayed the specials of the week was covered with a metal shutter and a huge drift of snow had blown up against the front door, a sure sign that it was no longer being used. Margret stared at it in disbelief, realizing, for the first time, how the weeks waiting for John had drained her and how much she needed to interact with other people. Deflated, she turned away and started walking back towards her grandmother's house. A wisp of smoke rising from the chimney at the back of the store caught her eye. There was someone there. Mr. White's smiling face, as he handed her change, flashed through her mind. He was such a sweet man! She looked into the yard behind the store. A path had been shovelled to the back door.

Margret opened the gate and hurried down the path, ringing the doorbell repeatedly when she reached the door. There was no response. "Oh," she paused and reminded herself, "the electricity is off." She began knocking, softly at first and then with heightened vigour as the door remained closed. Finally, she cautiously reached for the doorknob. It turned easily in her hand and the door opened before her. She stepped carefully through the doorway, not certain of what she was walking into. Was it a storeroom, or perhaps living quarters, for the Whites? She had never entered the store from this door before and had never considered exactly where they might live. The Whites were always in the store in much the same way teachers were always at the school. Their home lives meant nothing to her as a child.

It didn't take long to discover this was not their home. She had entered a storeroom, with rows of shelves with boxes of goods stacked on them. As she walked further into the room, she saw an open space with a small wood heater that was connected to a chimney. Behind it was a small table with an assortment of dishes and other kitchen items: a chair with a sweater thrown across it and a double bed covered with a mound of sleeping bags. A pail of half melted snow sat on top of the stove. Obviously, someone was living here.

"Hello. Mr. White?" Margret called out. "Hello. Mrs. White? Are you here? It's me, Margret. Martha Crawford's granddaughter."

There was no reply.

As Margret moved further into the room, she noticed the door that led into the store itself. She pulled it towards herself cautiously, calling out as she did so "Is anybody here?".

No one answered.

A thick quilt covered the doorway between the storeroom and the store. As she pushed it aside, and opened the door behind, a blast of cold air hit her face. It felt even colder it than it had felt outside in the wind, reminding Margret of how much heat one little wood stove could produce. She advanced further into the store, calling out as she did so. "Mr. White, are you here Mr. White?"

The store was dark, which was only natural considering that the large window was shuttered. As her eyes adjusted to the darkness, Margret could see that it remained much like she remembered it as a child. A convenient stop for those who lived in the neighbourhood to pick up the necessities of life and a safe place for children to spend their allowance on ice cream or Sno Cones in the summer and candy or chips in the winter. Even in the dim light she could see the line of glass jars near the cash register that housed the penny candy. How many times had she stood in front of them trying to make the perfect choice? They probably cost more than a penny now, she thought ruefully, what with inflation and all.

She turned back to return to the warmth of the storeroom and was startled to see the quilt move. A soft meow broke the silence and a large grey cat walked up to her and began rubbing itself on her leg.

"Mouser, Mr. Mouser, you're still here," she cried out as she knelt down and began to pet him.

He seemed to reply in the affirmative as he pushed his head against her hand with a loud rumbling purr.

"Come on Mouser, let's get to where it is warm!" she exclaimed. She pushed her way back into the storeroom and shut the door. She sat down on a chair allowing the cat to jump into her lap. The petting resumed.

As her hands stroked the soft fur of the cat, Margret realized that this couldn't be the Mr. Mouser that she had played as a child. After all, that would make him at least thirty-four years old, which was quite impossible. She also remembered that the Whites had adopted another kitten when she was in high school, one, who in time, replaced Mr. Mouser in the store. She had asked Mr. White why he called them both Mouser and he had replied that it wasn't a name, it was a job. She was the one who had added the Mr. to the front of the name when the kitten arrived. There were probably a lot of different Mousers, all looking exactly the same and called by the same name. "It doesn't matter," she murmured to the cat in her lap. You are the sign that the Whites are still here. We'll wait for them together."

As the moments passed Margret realized that she was getting very hot in her Grandmother's winter clothes and very carefully began to slip out of her boots and parka without disturbing the cat. As the jacket dropped from her shoulders the back door opened with a loud bang. She jumped to her feet crying out "Mr. White, I'm so glad you're here!".

But it wasn't Mr. White who came around the shelves with a load of wood in his arms. It was a young man of about twenty-five, whom Margret had never seen before. He seemed to be as shocked to see her as she was to see him. He dropped the load of wood by the stove and demanded loudly, "Who are you and what are you doing here?"

By this time, the cat had been unceremoniously dumped onto the floor and Margret was demanding herself "who are you and where is Mr. White?"

"Mr. White? Who is Mr. White??"

"The man who owns this store."

"Oh, him. Dead probably."

"What do you mean, dead probably?"

"Don't you know? Everybody is dead. Or, at least, almost everybody. Not everybody because you and I aren't. "

"Everybody's dead?" Margret stared at him in horror. "I know things haven't been working like they should. For instance, the electricity is off. But dead? How can that be?"

"I don't know all the details. It seems it started with a flu of some sort that was spread through the airports. It started killing people. And then they found a vaccine, which was supposed to stop it, but that was even worse. Everyone who took the vaccination died within a week, which was almost everyone, and of course, as they were doing that, they spread the flu to everyone else and so they all died too."

"But you, why didn't you die?"

"I wasn't in town. I was out at an oil rig when it all started. One by one the men left for the city. They never returned so I kept doing my job as long as I could. Finally, I was running out of food and drove into the city and found it basically deserted. I had a room rented in a friend's house, so I went there first. Everyone – the whole family – even the little baby, were lying in their beds, dead. Well, not the baby. He was in his mother's arms." He paused and wiped away a tear running down his cheek. "I couldn't stay there and I was hungry. When I saw the store, I realized there would be food inside, so I broke in. I have been living here ever since."

Margret continued to stare at him as he spoke, her mind racing as she put bits and pieces of what she knew together with what he was saying. The silence, the empty streets, the drifted in doorways, John's not arriving, the lack of electricity and the fact the Whites were not in their store. How else did anyone make any sense of this?

"You have their cat, Mr. Mouser," she stated, pointing at the cat at her feet.

"Yeah, I guess so," he replied. "He was here when I moved in. It's been good to have a little company. How do you know his name?"

"All their cats were called Mouser and all of them looked just like this. I added the Mister myself when I was a little girl. The Whites didn't mind. They said they thought it was cute."

"So, what about you? Why are you alive?" He turned and picked up a tea kettle and poured some of the snow water into it. He placed the pail on the floor and the kettle on the top of the stove. He opened the front and filled it with pieces of wood before he turned back to face her.

Margret drew a ragged breath, all the while aware that she needed to be cautious. She didn't know who this man was. She couldn't put her daughters in danger. "My grandmother died," she said. "Not from the flu, but just before this all started. I was her sole survivor. I came up for the funeral and to make the arrangements to dispose of the house and all its contents. My husband was on a business trip and so I came up alone. He told me to stay put. He's joining me here shortly. So, I have been going through the house trying to decide what is worth keeping.

This morning I was watching the snowstorm and I remembered how my best friend Natalie and I used to play a game we called Storm when we were children, so I came outside. When I was walking, I saw the store and remembered how much I liked the Whites, so I stopped to say hello. I saw the smoke coming from the chimney, so I thought they were here, but when I came in it was empty, except for the cat, of course. I'm sorry. I didn't mean to invade your privacy. I wouldn't have just walked in if I didn't think the Whites were here."

"No problem. It's not really my house, I guess. Just somewhere to stay as I try to survive this winter. It's been a miserable one."

"So, if you were out on the rig, how did you find out what happened here?"

"Folks told me. I've spent a lot of time wandering around the city trying to find people who were still alive. There was a whole gang down on Richmond Avenue. Vagrants mostly, you know the type, those who have drugs and alcohol as their top priority in life. Getting a vaccination was the least of their concerns. They wanted me to join them, but I'm not really into that sort of thing. They were camped out in the liquor store at that time. It was before the temperatures dropped so low. Haven't seen them recently. Who knows, they might not have survived the cold."

The kettle on the stove started whistling.

"Want some tea?"

"I guess."

The man took two cups from the table, dropped tea bags from the canister into each of them, and then carefully added the boiling water. "Sugar? Milk?" He picked up a can of carnation milk and poured a little in one of the cups. "It was frozen, but it doesn't seem to have hurt it."

"No thank you. I'll just have the tea."

"Okay. oh, I know, we can make this special." He opened the door to the store, lifted the quilt and disappeared inside. When he returned, he was holding a box of tea biscuits in his hand. "They might be a little bit cold, but they'll warm up fast."

Margret's mind raced as she sipped her tea and nibbled on a tea biscuit. The man was talking, something about growing up in New Brunswick and coming west to work on the oil rigs, but she couldn't concentrate on what he was saying. She was desperately trying to figure out how on earth she was going to be able to leave this room and get back to her grandmother's house without him following her. How had she managed to put herself in such a situation?

He stood up as he drained the last of the tea from his cup and set it on the table. He reached over and took the cup from her hand, placing it carefully by its mate. Then he took her hand and pulled it towards him saying "Come on, stand up. I want to look at you."

Margret dutifully rose, keeping a close eye on his face as she did so.

"Aaahh. It's been such a long time since I've been with a woman. Come on girl, give me a hug."

Margret's eyes widened. "No. I don't know you. And I'm married, you know."

"That doesn't matter. It's just a hug. I've been alone for such a long time."

She shuddered slightly as he wrapped his arms around her. As they stood holding each other she had to admit that this wasn't so bad. It was good to be held by a man again.

He groaned softly as he slipped his hands up under her sweater, softly caressing her bare back.

She stiffened and tried to pull away, but he backed her up against the wall, holding her tightly, murmuring, "Come on darling. You know you want it as bad as I do."

"No!" She struggled to free herself. "No! I'm married."

"Okay. Relax my darling. Just relax. It's all right. I won't hurt you. I know what no means. Just let me hold you for a little while."

As she stopped fighting, he eased his embrace slightly but continued to caress her back with soft strokes. She buried her face in his shoulder, hoping that he would relax enough so she could break free. It didn't happen. His hands moved upwards and she realized he was reaching for her bra. With one swift movement he had unhooked it, raised her sweater up over her breasts and pushed it aside to nuzzle her bare skin. She gasped as he caught her right nipple between his lips. Her body was betraying her. This felt so good. In the midst of trying to push him off, she wanted more, more, more. She felt him hardening against her pelvis as she arched her breasts up toward his face. It was as if he read her mind as he scooped her up and carried her over to the bed, dropping his pants to the floor before crawling in beside her.

The sex was intense but short lived. It was as if both of them were desperate to fulfill a need they didn't quite understand. Margret found herself responding in ways she didn't know she was capable of and climaxing at a level far beyond anything she had ever experienced before.

And then, just like that, it was over. They lay side by side on the bed panting. "Oh wow," she muttered. She stared up at the ceiling in complete shock as he turned on his side to face her and began talking.

It took a long time for her to register his actual words. He didn't seem to notice. Words about living together, of being like Adam and Eve in this brave new world where they were the only couple alive. How he would look after her; and, how she would bear his children; and, how they would create a new world, a better world.

She finally found the strength to speak. "I can't."

"What do you mean you can't? Of course you can! What else can you do? We don't have to stay in the store if you don't want to. We could go and find a better place. Maybe your grandmother's house if you would like to do that."

"No, I can't. I'm married. John is coming." There was no way that she was going to mention her daughters.

His eyes darkened as she said John's name. "I'm your husband now! Don't you understand. When a man and a woman come together like this, they are husband a wife. It's in the Bible."

Margret turned her face towards him as he ranted on. "You are going to stay with me even if I have to tie you up to keep you here. You are mine now. We have to be together."

She turned her eyes back to stare at the ceiling, realizing that she was going to have to be very careful. "Yes", she said softly. It is in the Bible, isn't it? I'd forgotten that. So, tell me again what we are going to do together."

The scowl on his face softened and he began to compare them to Adam and Eve again, creating a new world in which there would only be peace and harmony. Although she wasn't paying any attention to his actual words, she kept him talking by injecting a word now and then into the conversation; uh huh, I agree, why, how, and so on; thankful that she had learned to do this in a parenting course when girls were little.

Gradually his voice softened and finally stilled. Silence descended on the room. Margret looked over at him. He had fallen asleep She lay there motionless beside him as she tried to figure out what to do. She hoped that it was still storming outside. If she could slip out of bed before he woke up, get dressed and out the door before he realized she was gone, the wind would wipe out her tracks so that he couldn't follow her. They'd have to douse the fire in the fireplace when she reached home, so that he wouldn't see the smoke. It would be a dead giveaway that someone was living there. Would the girls understand? How much would she have to tell them? How she wished that she had not ventured out. She wasn't going to do it again.

He was sleeping deeply. Margret carefully lifted his arm that had been lying across her chest and laid it beside him. He stirred a little and then began breathing evenly again. She slipped slowly and carefully out of the bed, picking up her clothes as she did so. She stood quietly looking down at him for a few moments, to ensure he was still asleep, before she started pulling on her clothes. "So far, so good," she whispered to herself.

She moved slowly and silently across the room to retrieve her boots and her parka. As she raised her right foot to step into her boot, she braced one hand against the shelves to steady herself. It wobbled slightly and she snatched her hand back to avoid making any noise. Once she was fully dressed, she turned and looked at the shelves for a few minutes. They were solid, mostly constructed of two by fours, but they weren't connected to the floor. Could she use them to save herself?

In an instant she had made her decision. She ran towards the shelves, pushing them over as hard as she could. They fell forward, covering the whole bed. She turned quickly and dashed out the door, leaving it swinging in the wind as she fled to her grandmother's house through the storm.

16

Frank and Jim sat at the breakfast table, thoughtfully eating their bowls of oatmeal. Simultaneously they raised their heads and looked at each other. "Today?" asked Jim.

"It's time," replied Frank

"Yes, I think it is. It's not going to be easy."

"I know. But we have to do it sometime."

"Today."

"Okay."

Both men went back to finishing their breakfast. Neither of them had to provide any more details to this conversation. The unspoken words had been hanging in the air between them ever since they left the parking lot at Tim Horton's and made their way back to the farm. They had continued hanging there as they made the adjustments to their home necessary now that the lights, heat and water no longer appeared automatically or with the flip of a switch. The living room fireplace had become the hearth of the kitchen, as well as providing the heat for the house. Since John and Julie had rarely used it there wasn't a stockpile of wood available to burn. Thus, a portion of every day was spent scavenging for firewood.

Frank had rescued Mary's hens from the coop across the road, after he had built a makeshift home for them in one of the stalls in the barn. Thankfully, Peter had thought to put out a full sack of grain when he began to get sick, which had kept them alive after he had become too ill to look after them. Jim took care of the cattle every day while Frank fed and watered the hens. They were beginning to reward him with fresh eggs on a daily basis, now that the weather was warming up.

Jim had rummaged through the back of the pump house to find the pieces that connected the pump to the windmill on the roof. As he and Frank figured out what went where and hooked it all up, he couldn't help thinking about all the disputes he had listened to as child between his parents about this windmill. His father loved the past and had hung on to it, as long as he could, while his mother was only interested in the present moment, and how the neighbours would respond to whatever they were doing. As the wind caught the vanes and water started gushing into the cattle trough, John glanced up at the sky with a grin.

"Thanks Dad. You did good. "

Spring was finally on its way. The temperature had gradually risen during the last week of March and now only dropped below freezing in the early morning hours, if at all. The snow was melting and the runoff was beginning to fill the ditches. In no time at all, geese would be flying overhead and the trees would be sprouting their new leaves. This winter's calves were all doing well, which would have indicated a profitable year for John in the past. It would take a trip into the city to see what this might mean for their current circumstances. Today was the day they would do this.

It was a quiet trip that day with both men deep in their own thoughts about what they might find. This silence continued as they reached the highway and looked at each other. The only tracks in the melting snow were those that they had left on their last trip to town. As they reached the outskirts of the city, the silence in the truck was matched by that of the world around them. There were no people in sight. No traffic flowing past them. No movement of any kind. Only the empty buildings suggested that this had been a bustling city of almost seventy-two thousand people a couple of months ago. Grande Prairie had become a ghost town. The parking lots were empty. The shops abandoned.

Their feeling of despair grew deeper as they drove further into the city. Main street was as deserted as the outskirts had been. "I had a feeling it was going to look like this," muttered Jim softly. "But I so hoped it wouldn't."

"Me too," Frank replied as he reached up to wipe a tear off his cheek. "Do you think that there is anyone left alive?"

"I hope so. But it doesn't look very promising at this point."

They drove through the downtown core and further east into a residential section of the city, meandering from one street to the next searching for any sign of life. Their faces grew more and more grim with each passing block.

Marisa and Joelle were very worried about their mother. She hadn't been herself ever since she came back from her venture out into the storm. They had been so worried as the hours passed and she hadn't returned. They had almost decided they would have to go and look for her themselves, when she suddenly began beating on the back door.

Margret had refused to tell them anything about what she had seen or experienced since she returned, but they both knew that whatever it was, it bothered her. She had stopped eating completely, and her sleep was restless. They had basically closed off the rest of the house and lived in the living room after the electricity went off, to make the best use of the heat from the fireplace. Thankfully, Grandma had a whole cord of wood stacked neatly against a wall in the basement, which allowed them not only to stay warm, but also cook their food. However, sleeping together in such a confined space meant that they were intensely aware of their mother tossing and turning in her sleep, often crying out with garbled sounds that may or may not have been actual words.

In the beginning they were convinced that their mother had come down with the flu and that they were all going to die, but when the symptoms of vomiting and diarrhea, as described on the news didn't appear, they knew it was something else. But what? The only thing they were sure of was that this couldn't go on much longer or they would lose their mother.

Marisa had gone down in the basement to bring up more firewood when Joelle heard the car drive up and stop by the house. "Dad!" she cried out and rushed to the door to greet him. But it wasn't a car and wasn't her Dad. It was a crew cab that had paused at the stop sign on the corner and was now turning north and driving away from the house.

Joelle glanced back at her mother lying on the sofa. She told us to stay in the house until Dad came. She wouldn't want Joelle to go outside, but she had to. They needed help, and they needed it right now. She dashed down the steps and began running down the sidewalk after the truck, waving her arms and screaming, "Stop! Stop! Please stop!"

"We may as well give up," said Jim. "It's no use. There's no one here."

Frank turned to look at him. As he did so, a flash of movement through the back window of the truck caught his attention. He turned further see to more clearly, and began yelling, "Stop! Stop! There's someone coming after us".

Jim slammed on the brakes. Both men had opened their doors and leapt out of the truck by the time it came to a complete standstill. They ran towards the teenager who was running towards them with tears flowing down her cheeks. She threw herself in Jim's arms crying. "I didn't think you were going to stop. We need your help. We so need your help."

Jim held her close until she stopped shuddering. "It's okay. We've got you. Who are 'we'?"

"My mom and my sister and me."

"And, where are they?"

"Back there in my great grandmother's house." She pointed to house just as Marisa appeared in the doorway with the firewood in her arms.

"Well, let's go see them." Jim wrapped his arm around her shoulders steadying her with his body as they made their way down the sidewalk. "Frank, do you want to bring the truck."

"Sure thing," he called out as he turned back to retrieve it.

"I'm sorry Mom," Joelle cried out as they entered the house. "I know you didn't want us to go out, but you're so sick and we don't know what to do any more. These men will help us."

Margret sat up slowly, pulling her housecoat tight around her chest and stared with distrust at the two men who had invaded the room. "We don't need you," she said stiffly. "My husband is coming."

"Yes, we need them Mama," stated Marisa sternly. "You haven't been well since you went out into the storm. And as for Daddy, well he's been coming for months now and he still isn't here."

She turned to the men. "Welcome to our home. Would you like to take a seat? I can make some tea if you want."

"Yes, to the seat," said Frank as he closed door behind him, "but no to the tea. Not right now any way. I think that we had better get to know one another."

"I guess we can introduce ourselves first," said Jim, after they had all found themselves a seat. "I'm Jim Peterson and I run a cattle farm just west of the city. I lost my wife to the influenza in February and actually caught it myself, but due to my circumstances at the time, I managed to survive. We came into town today to see if anyone else had been as lucky as us, and here you are."

"And I'm Frank Sullivan," said Frank. "I grew up on the farm next to Jim and have been working as a doctor at the hospital here for the last ten years. I, too, came down with the flu, while I was at the hospital, and with Jim's help was able to survive. We thought we might have been the only ones who did, until I saw you running behind the truck." He turned to smile at Joelle.

"Well" said Margret stiffly, "I am Margret Ashton; and, these are my daughters: Marisa and Joelle. I grew up in this house with my grandmother, Martha Crawford. She died just before the flu outbreak of natural circumstances, and we drove up to make funeral arrangements. We have been living here in the house ever since, waiting for my husband to arrive."

"So, you didn't get the vaccination?" asked John.

"No," replied Margret. "Like I said. We are waiting for my husband. We planned to all go together, but he hasn't arrived. In the end, we missed our chance. I guess that was a good thing."

"So basically, what you're telling us, is that you haven't had the flu because you were never exposed to it."

"I guess that's it. John told us to stay in the house and so we did. We had lots of food on hand, and once the electricity went off, we were able to stay comfortable with the fireplace here. It's kind of fortunate that grandma preferred wood heat."

"Wow. That's a pretty neat story. But the girls mentioned that you're not feeling well."

"I don't have the flu if that's what you are worried about. I just don't have an appetite and haven't been sleeping well these last few days. I don't think it's anything to worry about. "

"Well, we do," Marisa cried out. She turned and faced the doctor. "She hasn't had a full night's sleep since I don't know how long. She tosses and turns and wakes up at times screaming. She hasn't eaten in days. We don't know what to do. We can't help her. We know she can't go on like this."

The girls looked hopefully at the men, who were looking at each other. Frank nodded slightly. Jim turned to face Margret. "We came to the city to see if there was anyone else alive. We haven't seen any signs, but then we almost missed you, so we might have missed others. You look like you are comfortable here so if you want to stay, that's okay. I do have a large enough house on the farm to have you come live with us if you want to. It's your choice."

"Thanks, but no thanks. We're staying here." Margret's voice was stiff and flat.

"I'm not," said Joelle." I'm going with them. He's a doctor and he can look after you much better than we can." She turned and headed towards the stairs. "I'll get my things."

"That's a kind offer" said Marisa." I, too, will take you up on it. So will my mother. She's afraid to leave the house in case my father shows up, but I don't think he's coming. If he is, we can make sure we let him know where we have gone so he can find us."

"Yes, we can post a note on the door with the directions. That's not so difficult." Jim turned back to Margret.

"We're not going to take you with us against your will." "Well, I'm certainly not going to stay here on my own. If the girls insist on going with you, I don't have any choice. I have to be there to protect them. Let me get dressed."

It didn't take long for all three to have their possessions back in their suitcases, sitting by the door. While they were packing, Jim had drawn a simple map to the farm. Above it he wrote, Attention: John Ashton in large letters. Your family is safe and living here. An arrow pointed to the location of the farm on a crude map. He taped it firmly to the door with packing tape as Frank helped the others load their suitcases into the box of the crew cab.

17

The ride back to the farm was a quiet one. Everyone was lost in their own thoughts as they drove through the empty streets. The reality of their situation was beginning to sink in.

The emptiness continued once they reached the highway, heading west out of the city. "It's not far now," Frank said as he turned to look at the Ashtons in the back seat of the truck.

"It's unbelievable," said Marisa softly. "It's like we are in the midst of a dream world. I never thought a city could be this still."

"A night mare!" Margret retorted. "A terrible nightmare, but one we won't be waking up from."

Silence returned to the cab as everyone nodded in agreement.

They turned south off the highway and headed down the side road towards the farm. A battered pickup appeared, parked at the side of the road. A large black dog was standing in the truck box, wagging its tail as they approached. Jim took his foot off the gas, pulled up alongside the other truck and stopped. Frank rolled down his window, matching the action of the other driver.

"Thank goodness you're here," the driver called out before Frank could say anything. We've run out of gas." "We can help you with that" Jim said, leaning forward to make sure his words got past Frank. "I'll be right back."

"Okay then, we'll be waiting."

Jim dropped off Frank and the Ashton's, along with their suitcases, in front of the house. He drove to the shed, where he ran in, got a jerry can, and then drove over to the fuel pumps. He keyed in the numbers on the key pad and began to fill the can with gas when the trigger on the hose was released.

As the gas ran into the jerry can, he looked up at the tanks, realizing for the first time how fortunate he was that he was living on a farm where people had access to fuel all the time. How did anyone get fuel at a service station without electricity to run the pumps? This was something he was going to have to discuss with Frank. And what's more, what were they going to do when they had used this fuel up? It wasn't like he could just make a call on his phone and a truck would appear as it had in the past. But first things first; the can was full, now on to rescue the travellers.

Frank entered the house with the Ashtons while Jim was getting the gas. He led them into the kitchen and opened the door to the pantry. "Everyone is likely hungry by now. I guess we had better get some food together. Do you want to help?"

Both girls nodded as Margret sank down into the nearest chair.

"Okay. I'll get the fire going in the fireplace while you find something in here." He gestured towards the pantry door. "There's not much left, but I'm sure we can pull something together. We heat it up on the fire with that pot," pointing to the one sitting upside down in the sink.

Marisa entered the pantry and started pulling out cans and handing them to Joelle. There wasn't much to choose from, as Frank had said, but they did come up with five tins of stew to dump into the pot. They weren't all the same kind but that likely wouldn't matter once they were all mixed together. They also found a jar of pickles and some crackers to go with the stew. They hoped it would do. They brought the pot into the living room and Frank carefully balanced it on the logs which were now ablaze.

 "I never had much to do with cooking with fire when I was growing up," he said "but you know, I'm getting pretty good at it, if I say so myself." He handed Joelle a large ladle. "You can keep your eye on this and stir it now and then so it doesn't burn. And you," he said turning to Marisa, "can find some plates and cutlery while I go out to the pump house to get some fresh water."

An hour later, everyone had finished eating and the dishes had been washed a put away. Frank filled the pot with water and then added a hot chocolate mix that Marisa had found in the pantry. Everyone settled down around the fireplace with cups of hot cocoa in their hands. It was time to get to know one another and decide what to do next.

Jim and Frank started off the introductions, in much the same way they had in Margret's grandmother's house and Margret followed their lead.

Then Samuel Burdock described how he, his wife Teresa and their children Caleb, Jacob and Sarah had ended up on the side of the road by the farm. "We have a quarter of land west of Albright. We were planning to go into Hythe and get the vaccinations like they told us to, but Sarah got sick and you know you're not supposed to vaccinate a sick child. It wasn't the flu or anything like that, more like a cold, but she was feverish and coughing so we decided to wait until she was well again. We thought we had lots of time.

A neighbour stopped by to tell us that the vaccinations hadn't helped; that everyone who got one was dying and so they had stopped giving them. Then the snow started to fall, and the cold hit and the storms followed. Finally, the power went off. We all stayed in the kitchen with candles burning to keep us warm until the temperature outside rose. It's amazing how much heat they give off. But then we were running out of food, so we decided we needed to come to the city for help.

As we passed Wembley, we realized that we weren't going to make it with the amount of fuel we had but kept driving as there wasn't anything else we could do. When we saw your tire tracks on the highway, coming off this road, we decided to come this way in hopes you would return. Thank goodness you did."

"And thank goodness you came into town and found us," interjected Margret. The tension was beginning to leave her face.

"Well, I'm thankful that we are all here together tonight," replied Jim. "I was beginning to think that I was going to be stuck here with just Frank for company for the rest of my life."

"Now that would be a disaster wouldn't it," Frank responded. Everyone laughed.

"And by the way, the dog out there is Buck. He's a good farm dog. I hope you don't mind us having him."

Sarah started yawning. Jim glanced at her and said, "It looks like it's time for bed. Margret – you and the girls can take over the master bedroom. Simon, your children can have my daughter's bedroom while you and Teresa can have the guest room. Frank, you can move to Kyle's room for now as it has a single bed, and I'll stay down here on the sofa. Is that okay with everyone?"

They all murmured their assent as they got to their feet and were directed to their various rooms.

It didn't take long for the house to grow quiet. As the flames continued to dance in the fireplace, Jim pulled his blanket up around his neck. His thoughts flew back to he and Frank sitting at the breakfast table together just a short twelve hours ago. "And now we are ten," he murmured softly. "We are not alone anymore." His eyes closed. He fell asleep.

18

The next morning Frank came downstairs with his doctor's bag in his hand. "I thought I'd give you a once over Margret and see what we can do to help what's going on in your body." Joelle jumped up from the table and threw her arms around his waist, while Marisa mouthed "thank you" to him from her seat.

Margret sighed as she watched the reactions of her children and slowly got to her feet. "Let's get it over with. Where are we going to do this?"

"I thought we might go into the back yard. It's an absolutely, beautiful day outside, and I can only do a cursory examination for now with what I have here. You won't have to take your clothes off or anything like that."

"Okay, a garden check-up will definitely be a unique experience." Together they headed towards the back door.

Fifteen minutes later, Frank and Margret were sitting side by side on the garden bench. He removed the blood pressure cuff from her arm, rolled it up, and placed it back in his medical bag as he talked. "Well, Margret, it's what I thought. There is nothing physically wrong with you, at least from what I can determine today. Your blood pressure is at a perfect level. Your heart is beating well; temperature right on; reflexes are good; and, there is no congestion in your lungs, by the sounds of things. I can't see any problems in your throat, your eyes or your ears." He paused for a moment to let this sink and then spoke again. "I expect that the loss of your grandmother and the stress of waiting for your husband, have just become too much for you to take right now."

Margret stared straight ahead for a few minutes as Frank sat quietly beside her, waiting for a response. Her lower lip began to tremble and she finally blurted out a few words. "No. it's not that. I just don't know what is going to happen to the girls when I'm in prison."

Frank blinked. "In prison?"

"Yes, in prison. I killed a man and when they find out, they will send me to prison."

She turned and gazed into Franks face, tears falling from her eyes. Suddenly, as if a dam had broken, the words started pouring out of her mouth. She told him about Natalie and how they used to play Storm. She told him about the Whites owning the store on the corner and their cat Mouser and how she had added the Mr. to his name as a child. She told him about the store being all closed up when she got to it and how she had noticed the smoke coming out of the chimney. She told him about going inside to wait for the Whites only to find out it wasn't the White's living there. She told him about the young man from New Brunswick; how they had sex; how he wanted to be Adam and Eve; and how she had killed him by pushing the shelves down on top of him while he slept.

"At least I think I killed him. The shelves were so heavy. I didn't stay long enough to find out. He didn't follow me or find the house. The girls insisted on using the fireplace, even though I was resisting. I just couldn't come up with a reason we shouldn't that made any sense to them. But it would have been a dead give-away of where we were living. When they find out, I will go to prison. "

It was Frank's turn to stare up at the sky, trying to formulate a reply.

"Well, I'm not sure who 'they' are, but I don't think we have created a prison system yet."

"Created a prison system? Of course, we have a prison system."

"No, we don't. You see Margret, we are not living in the same world that we were two months ago. All of the expectations, the rules and the institutions that we were living under are gone. It's all new and different."

He went on to describe the day that he and Jim had decided to go into the city to get coffee from Tim Horton's and the revelation they both had sitting in that empty parking lot: the revelation that the world had completely changed, and nothing was the same anymore.

"Everything that we were taking for granted is gone. There is no 'they'. There is only 'we'. We are in charge of what was going to happen from now on. You, me and the others sitting in that kitchen having breakfast."

"But I still can't go around killing people."

"No, you can't, and I expect that you won't."

"But I did."

Silence returned as they both stared off into space, lost in their own thoughts.

Finally, Frank began to speak again. "As I see it, there are two major forces at work here. The first one is consequences. For example, if Jim had not been invited to speak at that conference in Brazil, neither he nor Julie would have been in the airports; and, he would still have her at his side. However, I likely wouldn't be alive because he wouldn't have figured out how important it is not to sleep when that virus has its grip on you." He paused for a few minutes to let his words sink in. As he gazed out at the farmyard, the slow spin of the windmill caught his eye. "Here's another consequence. If Jim's Mom had won the argument about the windmill with his Dad, we'd have a lot more trouble providing enough water for ourselves and for the cattle. But she didn't, and because of that we have a constant supply of water."

"And if some damn fool hadn't decided to create that damn virus in his damn laboratory, none of this would have happened."

"Right, but what happened to you in the back of White's store is something completely different. It's another force to be reckoned with: one called survival. As a mother, the survival of your children was your main concern. You had to get back to them and you couldn't put them in danger while you did. You did what you had to do to survive. Survival. That's the main force we are going to be dealing with here on this farm. What are we going to have to do to survive?"

"Like a mama bear defending her cubs," murmured Margret.

"Yes, that's about it."

Margret quietly considered these words for a few minutes. In time she turned to look at Frank with shining eyes. "Oh, Dr. Sullivan, thank you. Thank you, thank you, thank you. I did do what I had to do in the moment didn't I? Oh, how I wish it had been different, but your explanation makes it so much more bearable." She stood up and stretched her arms towards the sky, letting her guilt fly free. "Shall we go and tell the others?"

"I don't think they have to know. You did what you did in the moment. It's over and done. If it made any difference to any of them, I'd say yes, but it doesn't. So, let's keep it between ourselves for now."

The rest of the group were sitting around the table discussing plans for the day. Jim was eager to get back into the city to see if there were any more survivors, while the Burdocks were more concerned with stocking up on food.

Marisa was taking notes as people threw different suggestions her way about what they felt was crucial.

"If we are going to drive around looking for people," Joelle said, "we have to make noise. Kind of like the Shriner's van was doing, urging people to go and get their vaccinations. I don't think I would have heard your truck if I hadn't been listening for my dad."

"So, just don't drive and look, but toot the horn too?" asked Jim

"Yes, something like that. Otherwise they might not know we are out there."

"Look for smoke coming out of the chimneys," Margret spoke up as she neared the table. That's a sure sign that someone is living there."

"Perhaps we should divide the city into sections, so that we won't waste time going somewhere that someone else has already covered. I think Julie had some kind of a map of the city for her work with the farmer's market." Jim got up and rummaged through the drawer of the desk as he spoke. "Yes, here in it is."

"And as for the food," said Frank, "we can just break into any of the grocery stores and take what we need." He looked at Teresa. "Maybe you and Margret can draw up a list of what you think we need for now. Jim and I have practically cleared out the pantry here, except for the oatmeal and the eggs we are getting from the chickens." "Our Dodge is full of gas. It's an SUV," said Margret. "We can stop at Grandma's and get it. It will allow us to cover more area."

"I've got a car too," said Frank. I was just too sick to drive when Jim brought me out here. I think there's gas in it."

Jim looked at Samuel. "We can fill your truck with gas. You can take Frank and the boys with you to get his car. I'll take the women with me for Margret's SUV."

"I don't know if I am comfortable with the women wandering around the city on their own," Frank said, glancing in Margret's direction. "Perhaps they can take care of the food, while we men look for survivors."

"That sounds like a good idea. There's lots of room in the our dodge. We'll probably be safe as a group of five. We can head back here and get something ready for you eat when you return."

As they were talking Jim was studying the map. "This should make things easier. All of the residential areas are marked in blue. Frank, why don't you start in the southwest corner in the O'Brien Lake area. Samuel can head to the northwest corner after he's dropped you off. It's called Royal Oaks, Samuel. I'll start on the central east side at Trumpeter Village and head south."

"I think we also need to put up a sign on the highway," said Samuel, "so if anyone is on the road like we were, they know we are here. I can take care of that if you want."

"Good plan. I've got to feed the chickens and check on the cattle to make sure they have enough hay and water, and then we can leave. Samuel, do you want to pull your truck up to the gas tanks? The combination is 4 5 4 5. Caleb, how about helping me gather the eggs."

As Jim stood up, he felt the depression he had been carrying since he and Frank sat in the Tim Horton's parking lot, slide off his shoulders. The day was off to a good start. Together they could build a community and start over again. In time, they would be reconnected with the whole world. Whoever had spread the virus was not going to win.

19

Margret pulled into the deserted parking lot of the Co-op store, stopping directly in front of the main door. The glass had been shattered, leaving only a metal frame to protect the building from the elements. "I hope whoever did that is long gone," muttered Teresa.

"So do I," Margret responded. "Are you ready?"

"Yes, let's do this."

The women looked in each other's eyes for strength for a minute, then simultaneously opened their respective doors and stepped out onto the pavement. In the meantime, Sarah had jumped out of the back seat and run into the store yelling, "chocolate!".

"Sarah, wait," they both gasped, as they headed swiftly through the door after her, with Marisa and Joelle on their heels.

At first glance the store looked exactly as it usually did except for a few boxes and wrappers littering the floor. It appeared that someone had been eating right off the shelves. They looked cautiously in all directions but couldn't see anyone. "Let's make sure we stick close together, just in case," said Margret quietly. "Marisa, can you get a cart?"

Sarah had already reached the candy aisle and was carefully considering her choices. The others joined her. "Pick one," said Teresa. "You can eat it while you shop with us." She took the list out of her pocket and began to read it out loud and then asked, "Should we start with fruits and vegetables?"

Joelle led them towards the produce section. "I can't wait to have some fresh fruit again. We ran out about a month ago." She rounded the corner and came to a sudden stop. "We can't eat this. It's all spoiled."

As she stared at the mounds of rotting fruits and vegetables spread out before them, Margret remembered Frank's story of the lesson he learned in Tim Horton's parking lot. This was what it felt like -- not being able to take things for granted. This was the reality of the world they were living in. She took a deep breath. "I guess we have to do things differently. Our list will be useless. Only a fraction of what is here in this store will be edible, first with the freezing temperatures and now the thaw. We will have to pick and choose carefully. The dry food should all be okay unless mice have gotten into it. I wouldn't touch anything that was canned or frozen."

"What about the chocolate bars?" cried Sarah.

"They should be okay."

Sarah smiled and took another bite from the one she was eating. Then she stopped and asked, "But how am I going to pay for this?"

"We don't have to pay," Joelle responded. "There is no one to pay. We will just take what we need."

Sarah frowned and looked up at her mother for confirmation. Teresa nodded and Sarah went back to enjoying her bar.

A deep feeling of desperation washed over Margret as the she moved cautiously down the aisle with everyone following close behind. So much food had gone to waste. Now that she was paying more attention, she could see bottles that had burst when they froze and cans that had strange bulges There was so much food that one didn't dare touch because of the threat of botulism. She hurried past the dairy section as the stench of the rotting milk and eggs filled her nostrils, trying to think coherently of what they could use. Flour, sugar, and salt should be okay, and things like pancake mix and cereals. But this wasn't going to keep them healthy.

"I've got an idea" Teresa called out, pointing at the swinging doors leading into the back of the store. "It might be different back there." As they entered the storeroom, they saw more shelves stacked with cases of canned goods which they wouldn't be able to us. However, Teresa was more interested in what was to their right. She approached the first of two doors and pulled on the latched handle. It opened into to a cold room where more vegetables and fruits lay in a state of decay and where cases of milk and cream had gone sour. However, not all was spoiled. The potatoes, carrots, onions, cabbage, turnips and beets appeared to have survived quite well, as did boxes of apples and oranges. "I was right, she stated. This room is designed to keep out the heat, but it also did the same for the extreme cold. Thank goodness for that. It should be the same for the freezer next door."

As Marisa looked around the room, she said "We have to careful. Let's only take what we need for now. The refrigerator isn't working on the farm and I'm not sure that they have a cold room. Things will probably last longer here if the door stays shut. We can come back and get more when we need it"

"Good thinking."

Everyone pitched in as they placed a variety of the vegetables and fruits in the cart. Then they moved into the freezer where everything was still frozen. "This isn't likely going to stay like this long without electricity, but Marisa's right about it lasting longer here for now. Let's just take a couple of packages of meat and some fish."

"What about some sausages for breakfast tomorrow? And here's a case of butter. We can use that."

"Score!" Joelle waved a package of ice cream bars in the air. There's a whole case of these."

"They won't last."

"Then we can enjoy them on the way home." She tucked a couple of the boxes into the cart.

As they left the freezer, carefully shutting the door behind them to retain its temperature as long as possible, Teresa looked around wildly. "Sarah. Where's Sarah?" She quickly reopened the door to the freezer but she wasn't in there. She wasn't in the cold room either or hiding between the shelves in the back room.

"The candy aisle!" said Marisa and sprinted off to check. It was as empty, as were all the other aisles in the store.

By this time the whole group had spread out over the store checking every nook and cranny, to no avail. They gathered together by the tills, shaking their heads as Teresa cried out to each of them, "Did you see her?".

"Well she's got to be somewhere. Is there a toy aisle?" said Margret.

"That makes sense. She always went there to pick out some little thing when I was shopping for groceries. It's not a whole aisle, just a few things over by the post office."

Marisa was already running towards the back of the store before Teresa had finished the sentence. Sarah was standing staring at the floor behind the post office counter. She turned and looked at Marisa, and then pointed at the floor.

"There's a man sleeping there," she said.

Marisa rushed towards her with her finger raised to her lips. She picked her up and ran back to the front of the store as quietly as she could, whispering, "We don't want to wake him up." She continued to whisper as she handed Sarah over to her mother "Quick! Let's get out of here. There is someone sleeping back there!"

They were all shaking as they stored the groceries they had picked out into the back of the SUV and strapped themselves into their seats. Margret spun the Dodge around as she backed up and then floored the gas pedal after turning onto the street that led to the highway.

As they reached the outskirts of the city, they all began to laugh with relief.

"That was close," said Marisa.

"Too close," Margret replied.

"Are you mad at me?" Sarah whimpered.

"No, of course we're not mad at you. We just want to keep you safe. Let's have some ice cream." Joelle ripped the first carton of revels open and handed them out. "I think we all deserve a treat right now."

20

The aroma of the fish soup, bubbling away in the pot, filled the house as dusk fell. Cooking on the fireplace was proving to be an interesting challenge, yet one at which they were succeeding. As a line of different vehicles pulled into the yard, Joelle realized that the table set for ten was not going to be enough. She started going through the cupboards to find more bowls and spoons as Jim ushered the new guests into the house. In the meantime, Marisa set out a variety of the crackers they had picked up in the store and Teresa returned from the pump house with a fresh pail of water.

Frank pulled Margret aside as he entered the house. "I checked on the situation at White's for you," he said quietly. "The back door was standing open, just like you left it, I expect. The shelves did the job. A corner caught him right on his skull and crushed it. He would have never known what hit him. He would have died instantly."

"That's a relief. Thank you."

"I looked around a bit for Mr. Mouser, but didn't I see him. Of course, with the door open, he could be anywhere now."

"Thank you again! You know, you're a pretty good guy."

"I try. Let's make this the last time we'll talk about this." "Good idea. Thanks again. Let's get out there and get to know the new members of our community."

That evening there were twenty-four gathered around the fireplace in Jim's living room, each with their own story of survival to tell. An old man, Jack Barton, clutched his cane as he described his decision not to waste a vaccine on him at his age. He thought It would be better to give it to the young'uns. Thus, he had stayed home during the blitz. He was expecting to die any day, as he had run out of food. It was quite a shock to hear Jim knocking on his door.

The head nurse from the hospital, Lucy James and her family, her husband Jake and their sons Bill and Lester, shared their story next. She had listened to Frank and left the hospital shortly after he had, arriving home just as her family were about to go and get their vaccinations. She had convinced them to stay with her to help keep her awake instead. They had done so, each taking turns by her side. One by one they had also come down with the flu and in time defeated it in the same way as she had, just by staying awake and living on ginger ale and sauerkraut.

Two ambulance drivers from the hospital also had to thank Frank for what he had told them before the administrator forced him out. Paul and Gareth had spent their time delivering the corpses to the crematorium as they waged their own personal battles with the virus. It gave them something to do as they fought to stay awake. Days of this twenty-four-hour effort ended up saving their lives in much the same way that calving had saved Jim's.

And then there were also two men from the funeral home, David and Patrick, who, like the ambulance drivers, had kept busy day and night disposing of the bodies as they arrived. Although they had no idea how beneficial this would be, they had stuck to the task, determined to protect their city in the only way they knew how. "We just did what we had to do."

The last to arrive were a young woman and her five children. Lily had followed Samuel out to the farm in her own car, as he couldn't fit everyone in his truck. She described how her husband had left to work on an oil well, just days before the mass vaccination was announced and had never returned home. She had lost her first baby to SIDS shortly after he received his 2-month DPT; and, although the doctors insisted that the vaccine had nothing at all to do with his death, she had never believed them. She had been "anti-vaccination" ever since.

"It was hard this time," she said, "as I knew people were dying and they were pushing it so much on television and on the radio. They were even announcing it on the streets with the Shriners van. I probably would have given in if had it lasted longer than it did. But now I am so glad it didn't," she said as she hugged her youngest daughter close to her chest. Like Jack, she admitted that she was reaching a point of desperation, worrying about how to feed her family without exposing them to the virus when she heard the horn of Samuel's truck outside. She had no idea how devastating the situation was and was absolutely stunned as she drove through the city.

Once the introductions were finished, Jim and Frank began to describe what their vision of a community based at the farm looked like. They shared their story of sitting in the parking lot at Tim Horton's and their realization that everything that they had taken for granted all their lives was gone.

"We have all grown up in a pretty incredible time," said Jim. "Everything and anything we ever wanted was delivered to us from all over the world. Do you want pineapples from Hawaii or fresh strawberries from California in the middle of the winter? No problem. A new cell phone from China? Here you go. Lights at the flick of a switch? Heat just by sliding the bar on the thermostat? And for many of us, all we had to do is speak and our request was filled. 'Television on,' and it turned on. Want to visit your relatives in Europe or go gambling in Vegas? Just jump on a plane and you're there in a couple of hours. You had to have the money to pay for these things all right, but even then, a credit card would do. We've all gotten so used to everything being at our fingertips, we don't really know how to live any other way. But we're going to have to. The deliveries have stopped. All the deliveries! It's likely the most noticeable with lights, etc. right now because the electricity is off, but we have to be aware that everything we use from now on will not be replaced. Will we survive? Definitely. But it is going to take a lot of hard work and cooperation."

As Margret listened to Jim, she wondered how many times she would hear this speech? How many times they would all share their stories with each other? Was this to become a nightly event? Were their whole lives going to focus on how each had personally survived the terrorist attack? Or would there come a day when something else would take precedence? She yawned. The heat of the fireplace was making her feel very sleepy.

"All I can say," Gareth responded, is that it would be a hell of a lot easier if we could get the electricity up and running again. I studied a lot about this after that movie describing what the world would look like without humans came out. Seems that there are different problems connected to the different types of sources of the electricity. For example, coal-powered and nuclear powered stations would shut down the first day that there was no one there to look after the plant. That didn't happen here, so we must be getting our electricity from something else. If that's true, it's a problem with the grid, not the source."

"Of course we are," said Trevor." We get it directly from the Bennett Dam up by Hudson's Hope. About three and a half hours northwest of here. That's why they built it back in the sixties. To provide power for this whole region. It's a massive place. One of the biggest man-made lakes in the world, if I understand it correctly. Got enough water stored behind it, that it would wipe out most of this province, including us, if the dam ever failed."

Jack nodded. "You're right Trevor. I remember when they were building it back in the sixties. There was a lot of fear back then about it failing. I can't remember for certain how much of the province they believed would be flooded, but I do know we'd be treading water here. It's stood firm for over a quarter of a century now so I expect we're all right."

"So, if we trace the lines back to the dam and find the break, we should be able to have all the power we want again."

"Are you suggesting that you know how to do this?" asked David. "Fix the line I mean?

"Well no, but I was hoping one of you would," Gareth replied.

"I certainly have no idea," said Frank as he looked around the room." Anybody here ever worked for a power company?"

There was a chorus of nos.

"So that doesn't appear to be an option," said Jim.

"Generators are. I think we should start a priority list and put generators on the very top of it." It was Paul who was speaking up.

"Good plan," said Frank. That and finding more survivors of course.

Margret's head fell forward, jerking her awake. She must have dosed off. She blinked her eyes, thinking back over the last two days she had gone through. Definitely days of extremes. They hadn't been easy. She excused herself and climbed the stairs to the bedroom she and the girls were sharing. As she snuggled into the pillow she realized that hadn't thought of John once throughout the day. "I'm sorry," she whispered softly. "I love you. Come quickly."

21

Samuel had his head buried under the hood of his truck as Marisa came down the steps of the porch with a pail in her hand. What's up?" she called out. "Having trouble?"

He raised his head to look at her and replied, "I don't know how long I am going to be able to keep this girl going. She's been getting more and more temperamental these last few months. I think I've solved the problem now. Could you get in the cab and turn the key for me?"

"Certainly." Marisa opened the door of the truck, reached in and turned the key in the ignition. The motor roared into life. She stepped back and joined Samuel at the side of the truck. "And now that we've accomplished that," she said with a grin, "let's go shopping."

"Go shopping? What do you mean? I'm supposed to be out with the rest of the men looking for more survivors."

"Well, it looks like you need a new truck, and I've had my heart set on a little red mustang for some time. Today seems like a good day to solve both those issues. Wouldn't it be nicer to be looking for survivors in a new truck that you can depend on?"

"I don't have enough money or even credit for a new truck and I'm pretty sure that you, at your age, don't either."

"Oh Samuel, don't be foolish! We don't need money. We're living in a new age. We can just go and help ourselves like we did with the groceries."

Samuel's eyes widened as he stared at Marisa. "Don't need money, hey?" He paused, biting his lower lip as he stared at the motor which was now rumbling softly in front of him. Taking food from the grocery store didn't seem wrong as they needed it to survive, but a truck? A truck worth thousands and thousands of dollars?

Marisa spoke again. "The lots at the dealers are full of them. They're only going to sit there and rot, you know. We may as well make use of them while we can. No one else is here to use them."

"Hadn't thought about it that way, but it still doesn't seem right to me."

"It does feel strange doesn't it. I know what it felt like yesterday when we left the Co-op without paying for the food we took. But there was no one to give money to. If it makes you too uncomfortable, I suppose you can write them a cheque for it and leave it in their office. I doubt it will bounce."

Samuel laughed and reached up to slam the hood down. "Okay! Let's do it."

"I'll be back in a second. I've got to bring a pail of water into the house and let Mom know what we're doing. I'm sure she won't mind. There's not that much for us women to do in there anyway."

Hours of discussion had gone on in the living room after Margret had gone to bed the night before. It hadn't taken much for Jim to realize that his ability to host everyone on the farm was impossible as he looked around the room. The house wasn't big enough to hold them all. Some questioned the wisdom of setting up a community outside of the city. There were those who wanted to stay in their own homes. Others didn't mind the idea of everyone moving close to each other but thought it best to take advantage of the large amount of homes they could access in Grande Prairie. A suggestion was made that perhaps they should take over one of the large hotels in the city. There would be enough bedrooms for everyone as well as an institution-sized kitchen complete with all the pots and pans, dishes, cutlery and so on required to prepare meals and conference rooms big enough for everyone to eat together. Others preferred the idea of living in the country, away from the constant reminder of what they had lost. Pros and cons of a variety of situations were suggested, explored briefly, and left to be mulled over. In the end, no definite decisions were made.

As dawn approached, the newcomers chose to get into the vehicles and head back to the city, each with a specific task to complete the next morning. The women on the farm would stay there to organize the house, cook supper and do some of the cleaning that had been neglected since Jim had returned from Brazil. Although Frank never mentioned what had happened to Margret, he was even more leery of sending the women back into the city after what had happened in the Co-op the day before. The children would all stay with them, taking a day off to play with each other with Jack present to monitor them. Lucy and her family would be in charge of bringing more food out to the house, now that their numbers had increased. Paul and Gareth were assigned to find generators. As soon as the electricity could be restored, at least to the houses that were being lived in, life would be much easier. David and Pat would collect large plastic storage bins to keep the dry foods in to protect them from insects and rodents. Jim, Frank and Samuel would continue to patrol the neighbourhoods, since they knew where they had stopped the day before. Everyone would meet back on the farm for supper to review the situation again.

At the moment, Samuel and Marisa were the only ones who were deviating from their assignments. He pulled off the street into the first dealership they saw on their way into the city. Huge signs advertised Chryslers, Dodge Rams and Jeeps. Marisa sighed softly with disappointment, but she could see the gleam in Samuel's eyes as he gazed at the line of Ram trucks, so she didn't say anything.

"So, what do we do now? Choose the one we want, I suppose; and then, go inside and try and find the keys."

"Perhaps it would be easier if we get the keys first and then use them to find which truck they fit in."

"Sounds good." Samuel opened the door and slid out of the cab. He reached behind the seat to pull out a crowbar.

"What do you need that for?"

"Doors are going to be locked. We're lucky some are made of glass so we can break our way in. I sure hope the keys are not in a safe. Haven't got a clue how to open one of those."

The silence of the morning was broken with the sound of the shattering glass. Samuel carefully reached inside to turn the lock and the pulled the door open. "Ladies first! And be careful where you step. Wouldn't want you to cut your feet."

Marisa's heart was pounding as she tiptoed over the shards of glass. What if someone was here? What if Jim was wrong about this being a new world? What if they got caught? No one appeared. The only sound she could hear was that of their own breathing and the crunch of the glass as Samuel followed her into the building.

"Wow!" Samuel gazed around the showroom with delight. "This is where they keep the cream of the crop. I wonder how one gets them out of here?"

"I don't know. We would probably need electricity to open the big doors at that end of the room and we haven't got that, right now. In the meantime, where would they keep the keys?"

"Sales manager's office is my guess."

As they worked their way towards the back of the dealership, they passed one small cubicle after another displaying the name of a salesman. Finally, they found a door with a gold coloured plaque with Sales Manager etched into it. The door was locked.

It didn't take Samuel long to break it open with the crowbar. Inside they found a large flat metal cabinet attached to the wall. It too was locked. Samuel was about to hit it with the crowbar when Marisa cried, "No wait!" She checked the drawer of the desk that took up most of the space in the room. "Here's a key."

Sure enough, it fit in the lock and the metal door swung open revealing lines of keys, each with a remote control and a paper tag with a number attached to it. Each row of keys was labeled with the different vehicles that were offered for sale. Samuel chose a number of keys from the Ram row and headed out the door.

As he pressed the buttons on each of the remote controls, the trucks in the lot responded. "What do you think?" he asked turning to Marisa?

"It's your choice," she replied. "After all, it's going to be your truck. What colour does Teresa like?"

"Good Idea. She's always liked gold. We'll take that one." He pressed the start button on the remote control and the engine started up, purring softly.

"I'm going to do a trade in," he declared. I'll move it out and park old Betsy in the stall where it was."

"And while you do that, I'll take the other keys back into the office and put them back into the cabinet."

"You don't want to pick out something for yourself?"

"No, like I told you before, I want a red Mustang. Believe it or not, this has been enough excitement for me today. I'll get my Mustang later, now that we know we can do this. Let's go and finish looking for survivors in the neighbourhoods you are working in."

They hadn't gone down many streets, without any response from the homes they passed, when they realized that the fuel gauge in the new truck was sitting close to empty.

"Shoot, I should have thought of that. We're going to have to gas up somewhere."

"We just passed the Co-op gas bar when we left the bypass. "

"We're not going to be getting anything from them without electricity."

"Duh! Everything needs electricity doesn't it."

"Well, there's lots of gas in my old truck. We can siphon it out and put it in here."

It was very late when Marisa and Samuel returned to the farm. It had taken time to find a jerry can and a hose to get the gas out of the old truck. Then they had decided that they should at least finish the one neighbourhood he had been assigned to check before they headed back. After finding no one, they had turned west. Samuel had decided to try out the four-wheel drive on a side road instead of returning by the highway. A couple of miles down this road they noticed a cow standing by a fence.

"That's a Jersey" Sam exclaimed. "Best in the world for milk if you want quality, not quantity."

"What do you mean?"

"Well they don't give as much milk as the other dairy cows, but it's richer. More cream you see. And the butter you make from that cream, so yellow and so tasty! It's the best. She looks like she's big with calf. I wonder what she's doing here all on her own?" He looked all around for any farm buildings but there were none. "She'll be a real boost for us once she calves. Fresh milk, every day. I can't wait!"

As he was talking, Samuel had pulled off to the side of the road and stopped. He reached over and opened the glove compartment. "Shoot, now's the time I wish I was in Betsy.

Got all my tools in her. Well, I guess we will have to make do. At least I hung on to the crow bar."

Sam waded through the remaining snow across the ditch and used the crowbar to pull the staples from the fence posts so that he could lower the barbed wire to the ground. Then he reached up and caught the cow by the halter she was wearing and began leading her towards the truck. She didn't resist.

"Now if we only had a rope or something like that."

"Will this do?" Marisa began to unwind her scarf from around her neck.

"Perhaps." He tied one end of the scarf to the halter and the other to the mirror on the passenger side of the truck. You can keep an eye on her as I drive.

"I've never been this close to a cow before."

"You don't have to worry about her. She's a real gentle breed. Nothing to be scared of. I just need to know if the scarf lets go."

He got back into the truck and began driving very slowly homewards as the cow ambled quietly beside them.

Marisa began to laugh. "You wanted to try this truck out for speed and now look at us. At least we know it can go at a snail's pace."

22

Frank stepped out of the front door of the farmhouse and walked towards his best friend. Jim was leaning his arms on the top rail of the corral, gazing at the herd of Simmentals that were milling around the barnyard.

"What's up buddy? You look like you are off in another world."

"Just thinking about things, Frank. Julie and I have been working our butts off for the last twenty years building up this herd. Longer than that actually, as we both started handling this breed when we were teenagers in 4-H. And now, I look at them and wonder, what for?"

"Well, they provided a pretty good income for you in the past, didn't they?"

"There's no arguing that, but that's the past. What use are they in this strange new world we are living in? Even if each of us managed to eat a whole steer this year, we would still have too many. But I just can't turn them loose or get rid of them some other way. They feel like a millstone around my neck. Even that Jersey cow that Samuel and Marisa dragged here is of far more use than these are."

He turned and looked directly at Frank with tears filling his eyes. "On one hand I have to look after them for Julie. After all, they are all I have left of her. And on the other hand, why? They just aren't important to anyone anymore."

"You know we all support you, Jim. We all know this herd is important to you. I can't speak for the others, but I, at least, don't mind helping you keep them here."

"I know that. And I appreciate it. I just wonder if it is worth the effort. If it is, it's time to make some decisions. First of all, we need to castrate all of the male calves so that their meat is edible. Secondly, before we do that, we have to choose one of them to raise as a bull.

We sold the bulls last fall with the intention of getting some fresh blood into the herd. We actually made a couple of deals with breeders in Wyoming and Texas while we were in Brazil. What with the virus and all, they're not likely to arrive. It doesn't really matter this spring, but one also has to plan for the future. So, what do you think? Which one of the calves looks like good bull material?"

Frank carefully scrutinized the herd and finally pointed at one of the calves. "That one".

"You're not of much use. That's a heifer."

Frank chuckled. "I know. I haven't left the farm that far behind me! My question is, what does it matter? If we are only going to raise cattle for meat, won't any one of them do? After all, they're all top-notch animals."

"The bull is the most important animal in the herd if you are going have the best animals. I'm so used to working for the best, I don't know how to relax and do it differently anymore."

Jim sighed heavily as he continued to stare at the cattle. Finally, he turned to Frank again and said, "I know what I am going to do. I'm going to let the children choose. Julie would be absolutely scandalized if she knew, but that doesn't matter anymore. You're right. It really doesn't matter which one we keep as long as we keep one. The children can do it."

That evening, Jim brought up the situation with the beef herd as one of the priorities that had to be dealt with. He shared how the herd had been built up over the years and how he and Julie had sold the bulls last fall with the intention of bringing new ones in this spring. Although the arrangements had been made, he doubted that the bulls would arrive, considering the circumstances. He told of his decision to let the children choose the male calf that would be allowed to grow up and become the bull for the herd. Due to the number of cattle in the herd, he had also decided that they didn't have to worry about breeding the cows for a couple of years. There were plenty of calves to provide all the meat the group would require for some time. He added castrating the bull calves on the list as one of the jobs to volunteer for the next day. Everyone signed up for it.

Jim had no idea how hard his grief would hit him the next morning. Rubber boots were the top fashion accessory of the day, as everyone gathered by the corral. Although the snow had melted at this point, the ground had yet to dry completely. It was sure to be one messy job. Jim rummaged in the closest for his families' boots and handed them to Margret, Marisa and Joelle. "You may as well have these. Not much use just sitting here in the closet." He turned away quickly so that they wouldn't see he was on the verge of tears.

Outside in the barnyard, the children waited patiently. They were absolutely delighted to have the honor of choosing the bull. Although Lily decided that April and Candy were too young to go into the corral, in no time the other seven were walking between the cows, intently observing each of the calves and discussing the possibilities with each other. In the end they chose a brown calf with a white shawl across his shoulders and a white spot on his forehead which looked slightly like a heart, if you looked at it from the right direction.

As Jim and Samuel herded the calf and his mother into the barn, he had to admit that they had done a good job. He was sure that Julie would agree. His eyes threatened to overflow again. He steeled himself to keep them in check as he returned to the barnyard. The children ran towards him and announced that they had decided to name this calf Julian, if he agreed. He could not hold the tears in any longer and turned away. Had he not, he would have realized that he wasn't the only one crying.

Although the majority of the group had not any experience with cattle in the past, their sheer numbers helped the job move along smoothly. The first step was to separate the cows with heifers from those who had bull calves and move them out into the big pasture. This isn't something that Jim would have done in the past, as castration day was also combined with giving vaccinations and inserting ear tags which were used to keep track of the animals. The heifers would have also gone through the cattle squeeze to receive those, but vaccinations were the last thing Jim wanted to deal with this year. Ear tags had become meaningless.

Once the heifers were cleared out, the more difficult task of moving the bull calves into the small corral with the cattle squeeze at the far end began. Although they were only planning to separate the cows from their calves for a short period of time, the mothers didn't know this. They began to resist going in the direction they were being herded in spite of the line of humans in their way. Once their calves were no longer at their sides, they began to bellow, calling their babies back to their sides. This harsh cacophony increased in volume the longer they went without their calf by their side.

One by one, the bull calves were herded into the cattle squeeze. As Jim held it tight against their bodies, Frank swiftly slit open the scrotum and removed the testes. As the bucket at his feet began to fill up, the men began to joke about taking the prairie oysters into the kitchen for the women to prepare for supper, but in the end, no one actually carried it out.

This job took less than a minute. As Trevor slid the back gate of the squeeze open, Jim released the sides and the calf bounded free to rejoin his mother. In the meantime, the others were already herding another calf into the front of the squeeze.

By 5 PM the task was complete and silence had returned to the herd. Samuel opened the gate to the large pasture, allowing the cattle to roam out of the barnyard, which had been their home for the winter. High fives and congratulations on a job well done filled the air as the group members returned to the house for the evening meal.

That evening, as everyone gathered around the fire pit in the back yard, they discovered that the day spent working closely together as a team had shifted them in some way. Somehow, the priorities list didn't seem to be quite as important. Conversation drifted off in new directions.

"I think the worst thing about this whole experience is the 'not knowing'," said Margret, as she sat staring into the flames. "Not knowing what happened to John. Not knowing who created the virus in the first place. Not knowing who chose to put it in the airports and why.

"I agree," Trevor responded. "Not knowing what is going on anywhere but here," added Trevor. "Not knowing if there are other groups like ours out there in the world right now."

"I'm sure there are," said Frank, "somewhere, somehow; but, not knowing how to connect with them is frustrating."

"What I would like to know is whether that Pierce Paxton guy knew that his vaccine was going to kill everyone and is still living, who knows where, with all his billions, or if he took it too and died with the rest of them?" Paul retorted.

"Well the money wouldn't do him much good if he did know. Have you noticed one of the few places we haven't paid any attention to, as we focus on survival, is the banks?"

Everyone chuckled. "Yeah, money would do us a lot of good, wouldn't it? Maybe we could use it to start a fire."

"I remember reading about a virus that was supposed to be able to wipe out everyone," said Lily. "It was back in 2009 or so, I think. The article was about an interview with the scientist who had developed it. When the reporter asked him why he would do such a thing, he said, 'Because I can. I have the ability'. Seemed like a ridiculous reason at the time if you ask me. But it's even worse now."

"I wonder if that was Pierce Paxton."

"I don't know. I don't remember his name, and, of course, it was an article so I didn't hear his voice."

"What a voice, said Margret. It was so amazing!"

"I miss the evening news," said Teresa. "The feeling of being connected with the whole world and knowing what was going on in other places. Seeing the devastation caused by hurricanes and earthquakes, praying for those involved, in the midst of being so thankful it wasn't happening to me."

"And Facebook," said Lucy. "I didn't have much time for it but being connected with family and friends all over the world every day was such a joy. Celebrating births and weddings and graduations in ways that we hadn't been able to do before. Even being able share the sorrow of someone's passing was a gift. We've lost so much!"

"A lot of it was fake news both on the television and on Facebook," said Gareth, "meant to keep us in our place."

"I know that," Lily responded, "but I even miss that. Trying to figure out what was real and what wasn't."

"Well none of this surprises me. I know for certain that the elites in the world have been planning to wipe out most of the human population for a long time. That's why they were creating viruses in the labs. They are all probably celebrating, as they live in luxury in some spot that they had already readied before the virus was released. They probably haven't a clue that some of us survived." Gareth took a deep breath and opened his mouth to continue.

Paul spoke first. "We are quite aware of your conspiracy theories, Gareth. Who knows, they might be true. But the reality is, what we believe and what we actually know, are two very different things. Stating a belief as fact is as fake as anything else."

Gareth glared at Paul and began to rise out of his seat.

Jim held out his hand. "Easy now. There's nothing to get too excited about."

The sound of human voices was replaced by the crackle of the fire for a few minutes. Finally, Teresa broke the silence. "What interests me even more than not knowing, is the 'what ifs'. What if John had arrived in time for you to get vaccinated Margret? What if," turning to Lucy, "you had followed conventional wisdom and stayed in your bed in the hospital? Or in our case, what if Sarah hadn't had the sniffles?"

"Franks calls them 'consequences'," said Margret, glancing over at him with a smile.

"Yep," Frank responded. "All of those things that affect us on a daily basis that we may or may not have any control over. It doesn't matter if it was a choice we made ourselves; or if it was something that someone else did, perhaps even years ago, we end up living with the consequences."

"Aren't consequences considered negative Frank?" asked Jack. "That's how I was taught as a child. If you do this, or don't do this, you are going to suffer the consequences. They're something to be scared of. For example, if you smoke you will get lung cancer."

"They can be negative, or they can be positive. For example, if you plant carrot seeds in a garden, one of the consequences is that carrots will grow. If you look after the garden, you will have carrots to harvest. That's a positive. However, if you neglect the garden by not watering it or letting weeds choke out the plants, you won't have a very much to harvest. That's a negative. Same carrots, different consequences, depending on the circumstances. All of us here have specific consequences that put us on this farm in this moment. I think we can say that is a positive, considering the alternative."

"My big 'what if?' is about Julie." said Jim. "And I want to thank you all for the effort you put in today working with her herd. I'm sure she is looking down on us with gratitude tonight. I spend so much time wishing I had never taken her to Brazil through all those airports. But you know, if we hadn't done that, we would have lined up for the vaccination just like everyone else did, and I wouldn't be here either."

"And neither would I," Frank responded softly, "if you hadn't been there to teach me."

"Or I," Lucy chimed in.

"All of us, Mom." It was Bill's turn to speak up.

"And when you think about it Jim," said Samuel, "it was the herd that kept you alive. You had to stay awake for the calving."

Silence descended on the group again as they somberly stared at the flames dancing before them. They were all caught up in their own thoughts, reviewing the different circumstances that had brought them to this particular time and place. The circumstances that had allowed them to survive when so many had not. The circumstances that were either going to ensure their continued survival or perhaps stand in their way. One by one they quietly stood up and headed off to their beds, still deep in thought.

23

Margret was sitting on the front porch of the farmhouse playing Free Cell on her iPad. She was so thankful that she could charge up it again and was surprised at how much she had missed playing computer games throughout the weeks without electricity. However, she had to admit that this wasn't all about playing a game. In the midst of moving the cards across the screen there was faint hope, deep inside, that Face Time would suddenly come on, and John's face would fill the screen. How she ached to see him again. How wonderful it would be to hear his voice explaining what had happened to him and that he was still on his way. Her brain told her that she was being delusional, that this was impossible, but her heart wasn't willing to give up.

The cards began fall off the screen indicating another game had been won. Margret glanced at the watch on her wrist, laid the iPad aside and headed into the kitchen to check on the bread rising on the counter. She had immediately volunteered for this task when it came up during the previous night's meeting. Making bread was something her grandmother had taught her as a child. All the steps of measuring, mixing and kneading brought back wonderful memories of working side by side with her grandmother, as well as a feeling of satisfaction of a job well done.

Teresa had volunteered to help out with the bread making but Margret had declined. "You mentioned that Sarah and Jacob are going through a growth spurt and need new shoes and longer pants. Why don't you take the whole family into town on a shopping trip?"

"Thanks," Teresa replied. "What do you think Samuel?" turning to look at her husband.

"Sounds good to me." He reached over a squeezed her hand.

"You might want to take along a couple of the plastic bins and fill them with larger sizes too. This won't be the last time the children need bigger clothes."

"That's a good idea. As Jim says, 'The delivery trucks aren't coming'. When I think of it, I know it will be nice to spend some time on an outing with just our family for a change. You're sure you can handle the bread on your own?"

"No problem," Margret responded out loud, while silently thinking how much she was looking forward to having the kitchen all to herself for a change. She wasn't aware of what had made such a shift in her way of reacting, but the discomfort she had dealt with all her life when alone had completely vanished. Maybe it was a sign of maturity. Maybe it was spending so much time in the group. It really didn't matter. Being all alone working in the kitchen or sitting on the front porch enjoying the quiet of the countryside had become a real treat.

The bread loaves had risen nicely and were ready for baking. As Margret pulled open the oven door a heart shattering scream broke the silence. "Marisa!" Margret turned swiftly and ran through the door and down the steps heading in the direction of the old wooden granaries. They were being turned into storage sheds for all the dry goods that were being brought out to the farm.

Last night Marisa, Patrick and Paul had volunteered for the task of building shelves to store the bins on. Margret wasn't the only one responding to the scream. Patrick appeared in the doorway of the far granary while Joelle sprinted across the yard from the chicken house. Jack hobbled out of the door of the barn where he had been tending Caroline, the name he had given the Jersey cow, in memory of his wife.

Patrick and Margret reached the door of the nearest granary where the blood curdling scream was emanating from. He paused slightly, allowing her to enter first. She dashed through the open doorway and came to a sudden halt, blinking rapidly as she tried to get her eyes adjusted to the dim light. Paul was huddled in the corner with his hands covering his face while Marisa continued the blood curdling scream, all the while frantically pounding his back with her fists.

Margret stepped forward cautiously and touched Marisa's back. "I'm here," she said softly. "Hush my baby. Everything's going to be okay." Marisa's arms fell to her sides. She turned and fell into her mother's arms, sobbing hysterically.

As Margret held Marisa close, she glared at Paul over her head. "What did you do?" she hissed.

"I don't know what happened," he responded. We were working and everything was going well. I had just cut this board and brought it in. I needed Marisa to help me hold it in place, but she was lost in thought like she is so often. I reached out and touched her wrist to get her attention. She let go with this banshee wail and started scratching my face before I had any time to react. I tried to stop her by grabbing her wrist but that only made things worse. I didn't mean any harm." As he moved out of the shadow everyone gasped. Long streaks of red covered his face.

"It can't be that simple. You must have done something. Joelle, please help me take Marisa to the house. And as for you," she said, turning back to Paul, "We'll let the group decide what to do with you when they get back."

Marisa continued to sob as the trio made their way back to the farmhouse and up the stairs into the bedroom. They lowered her onto the bed. Margret bent over and gently removed her shoes and her jacket and then moved her into a reclining position so that she could cover her with the blankets. Joelle brought a chair and placed it beside the head of the bed. Margret sat down and took Marisa's hand in her own. She found herself rocking back and forth as she sat, in much the same way she had rocked Marisa when she was a baby. Finally, the sobbing subsided and with shuddering sigh, Marisa closed her eyes in sleep. It was another half hour before Margret reluctantly slipped her hand free and left the room. As she quietly closed the door she leaned her head up against it and whispered, "Oh John, I wish you were here to help me."

The bread had continued to rise on the kitchen counter and was now slopping over the sides of the tins. Margret closed the oven door and began dumping all the loaves back into the mixing bowl. "It's lucky that bread dough is so forgiving," she murmured as she began kneading it again. "Hopefully you will end up as good as you were before. Whatever. It will have to do."

It was a very somber group that gathered in the living room of the farmhouse that evening for the group meeting. The events of the day had been quietly passed on from one person to another as they arrived for the meeting and discussed between each other in private. However, now that they were all gathered together in one room, no one was saying anything. Marisa was still asleep upstairs and Margret had no intention of allowing anyone to wake her up. Memories of what had happened to her in Wright's store had plagued her throughout the day. She still didn't understand what had happened in the granary, but she was pretty sure that Paul had tried something sexual in nature.

Paul slumped in the corner with his hands covering his face. He knew that everyone was watching him furtively, thinking the worst of him. He didn't blame them. He would be thinking the same if this had happened to any one of the other men. In the midst of that acknowledgement came a deep sense of frustration. He honestly didn't know what he had done wrong.

Jim finally broke the silence. "Well Paul, I think you had better explain yourself."

Paul straightened up, dropping his hands down into his lap. Everyone gasped as the deep scratches were again revealed. He began to speak, telling exactly the same story that he told Margret and Patrick in the granary. A murmur began to rise throughout the room.

"Come on Paul. Who's going to believe that crap," cried Joelle. "Marisa wouldn't do something like this without a reason."

"Yes Paul. Tell us the truth." This time it was Margret who spoke up.

"He is telling the truth," came a voice from the doorway. It was Marisa. "It happened exactly like he said. I'm so sorry Paul," as she turned to look at him. I hurt you so bad."

The murmur in the room grew louder as everyone began commenting on what they had just heard.

Jim held up his hand "Quiet everyone!" He turned to Marisa. "You had better explain yourself."

"No, I will do it," said Margret, as the reality of the situation dawned on her. I think I understand." She went on to describe what had happened to Marisa and her friends just before they had come to Grande Prairie. Everyone listened intently.

"So, the touch on your wrist made you flash back to what happened in Minneapolis?" Lisa turned to Marisa to ask the question.

Lisa was a psychologist who had arrived at the farm just a few days before with her husband, Darren, and daughter, Susie. They were living out in a cabin on the lake when the virus outbreak occurred. Lisa was working on her thesis for her PhD, and Darren had accompanied her to look after their daughter, as well as do all the housekeeping as she wrote.

Trevor and Lucy found them in the Save-On parking lot, in shock, as they dealt with their return to an empty city.

"I guess so," Marisa whispered, "but it wasn't like I wasn't already thinking about it. I think about it all the time. Paul said I was lost in thought. And I was. I was thinking about that day, wondering what would have happened if Jeanne hadn't called the police. Wondering what they wanted to do with us. Wondering if the police had ever caught them. If the DNA they took from my fingernails was useful? If this whole fiasco with the virus and vaccinations just put everything on hold. I can't get it out of my mind."

"But why haven't you said anything?" cried Margret "Why were you carrying this all by yourself?"

"Because Dad told me to. That's what he wanted to talk to me about that night. He told me that it was over and done with, and that I had to forget it and get on with my life. He said that I shouldn't bother you with it, because you already had enough on your plate with grandma dying. He said you were weak and that he didn't want you worrying about this too. That I was strong enough to handle it on my own."

"And you reacted in a far stronger way than you did when the first incident happened?" Lisa continued on, as if she hadn't heard Margret's question.

"Oh yes, look at his face. Oh Paul, I am so sorry!"

"And this," said Lisa, as her eyes surveyed each person in the room individually, "is another example of dealing with survival. Who knows what would have happened to Marisa and her friends if the police hadn't intervened. None of us know. We can only guess, all the while being extremely thankful that we don't know because it didn't happen."

"In the midst of this, Marisa is now tuned to reacting strongly whenever she is put back into a similar situation. Our memories are stored through sensory input. In other words, the touch on the wrist triggered the memory, and her need to survive triggered the reaction. We've all got this. Memories stored through sensory input, and reactions ready at a moment's notice to ensure our survival. It's not just about Marisa and what she went through. It's about all of us.

"I'm afraid your father was wrong," she said turning back to Marisa. "When it comes to the need to survive, it's never over. Yes, it is in the past, but your brain will retain the input that you received from your body as protection. That's why it is so good to talk about it. Much of what you are dealing with now never happened. It's what you have created in your imagination as 'what ifs'. In time the 'what ifs' can become as powerful as reality. That's why it is so important to talk these things over with other people. It gives us the chance to determine what is real, or in other words 'acute'; and what we are creating in our mind. We call that chronic anxiety. In the meantime, if you ever have someone touch you un-expectedly on your wrist, you may have another extreme reaction like you did today. I'm pretty certain that it won't be as severe as it was today because you have let your fears out in the open, but it still might happen. If it does, don't feel bad about it. Just thank your body for ensuring your survival."

"Wow," said Lucy, "I know what you are talking about. When I was about five we went to the farmer's market. I remember that it was spring. My mother bought a pot of hyacinths that were blooming. They were purple and pink.

She let me hold them in the car as we were driving home and I buried my face in them because I loved the smell so much. We were t-boned by another car that ran a red light, and I ended up in the hospital for a long time because I was hurt so bad. Now every time I smell hyacinths I freeze. I can't move. No one has ever explained this to me before."

"It happens to me too" said Margret. "It's the lights and sirens of police cars that trigger me. They were going when the social worker told me my parents had died in the car accident. I freeze like you do Lucy and then I am overcome with grief for the next few days. My therapist called it a flashback. I never thought of it as a means of survival before."

Samuel cleared his throat and slowly began to speak. "This is kind of embarrassing. For me it's chickens. You might have noticed that I have managed to stay completely away from the chickens since I arrived. I think I was about four when I was visiting my grandparents. They had this big old rooster who was as mean and ornery as they come. Well, I was out in the yard one day and this rooster came after me. I started running and I tripped and fell. He was right on top of me before Grandma hit him off with her broom. I've been terrified of them ever since. Just want to start running every time I see one. And like the others, I have never thought of it as a survival issue before. I just thought I wasn't man enough to face something as small as a chicken!"

"At age four that rooster was probably close to the same size as you were. And their beaks, ugh, all ready to peck holes in you." Lily shivered.

"There are three responses in all, said Lisa. They all start with f: flight, fight and freeze. Marisa fought, in much the same way as she did when the men first grabbed her. Freezing is also common, but one might also find that they are running away. I think the reaction depends on the specific situation."

"I think we all carry something from the past," said Jim. "It was malls for Julie. She lost Kyle in West Ed when he was little. She refused to shop in a mall after that."

"Dogs for me. Bitten once and needed stiches."

"For me it's rats and mice. I have no idea why, but they terrify me."

"Horses. Used to love them, and then I got kicked, and now I am ready to run whenever they are close to me."

"Water, almost drowned as a kid. Even a bath tub is too much at times so I just use a shower."

As each person spoke up, the others were reminded of situations they had experienced and continued to react to. "The crazy thing about this," said Samuel, "is that no one teaches us this kind of information when we are growing up. Instead, they treat us like we are broken and need to be fixed."

"Or babies who need to grow up," injected Teresa. "We were given the message that you just need to use your willpower, and if you don't, well, that just shows the world how weak and useless you are. So, we go around pretending we are okay."

"And never talk about it because we don't want to appear weak," whispered Marisa.

"And in doing so, we cheat the world of who we really are, deep down inside," stated Frank softly.

An uncomfortable silence enveloped the room as each remembered how they had mistreated others in the past, defining them as weak or broken.

Gareth cleared his throat. "It's getting late. This is all sweet and touching, but can we get back to what we are really here for. What's up for tomorrow? Most of us have to drive back to the city, you know."

Margret looked at Lisa and mouthed the word flight.

Lisa smiled and nodded as her lips formed yes.

"Is that okay with everyone?" Jim asked as he picked up the priorities list. "Are we done with this lesson on survival? I certainly learned something I had never knew before. Thanks Lisa, Frank, and you too, Marisa. Not quite the way you would have liked to share it, I'm certain, but it has taught us all something. I know for certain I won't be judging another quite as quickly when they react in ways I don't understand. I'll be wondering what happened to them in the past."

A murmur of assent ran throughout the room.

"Okay, well then, let's move on with the business of surviving tomorrow."

Sleep didn't come easily that night for Margret as she lay under the covers. She couldn't help thinking about John telling Marisa that she was weak. Why would he do that? Yes, she had to admit that she had relied on him for many things that she could have done herself, but wasn't that what being the man of the family entailed? But weak? Too weak to be there for their daughters when they needed her? No way! Perhaps she didn't have the relationship with her husband that she thought she had.

24

There wasn't much room to move behind the counter. Trevor, Pat, Frank and Samuel stood staring at the bikini clad blonde lounging on the beach while Paul, Gareth and Jim leaned forward across the counter to get a better view. However, it wasn't the woman they were staring at. It was the white box across her torso in which a cursor blinked off and on beside the word password.

"It can't be that difficult," said Pat." After all, it has to be something that everyone who worked here knew by heart." He reached forward and began typing Husky on the keyboard. The screen blinked as a response appeared. "The password you entered is incorrect. Please ensure that you enter the correct password for this location." "Nope. Has anybody else got an idea?"

"You better not try that too many times," said Paul. "It might lock us out completely."

"Perhaps it's posted somewhere, especially if it is changed regularly." Gareth began looking closely at the bulletin board behind the other men's heads while the men behind the counter bent over to peer into the shelves below it. In a back room the generator rumbled, feeding the service station with electricity.

It had been such a simple plan. When Jim realized that the gas in the fuel tank on the farm was low, the decision was made that they would all meet at the service station with a generator, turn on the power and fill up their trucks from the pumps. They had become very proficient using generators to feed the electrical systems in all the buildings that they were living or working in, so it shouldn't be a problem. And it didn't appear so at first, as the lights came on and the coolers began to purr once the generator was going. But it didn't have any effect on the pumps themselves. They stood silent and unresponsive, in spite of the electricity that was flowing.

Their first thought was that there must a switch somewhere in the building that turned them on. They had diligently searched, flipping every switch they found to no avail.

Samuel shook his head in frustration. "You would think that one of us would have actually worked in a gas station at one point or another in our lives, considering how necessary they are to our vehicles. There's got to be an answer here, somewhere."

It was Trevor who suggested that perhaps they should try the computer. So much of the world was run by computers these days. Perhaps there was a program on it which would turn on the pumps. But now they had no way of knowing. They were stymied by a lack of a password.

Jim turned and headed out the door to survey the scene before him. Their trucks were lined up at the pumps waiting to be filled. In each box were several jerry cans used to refill the generators. No gas, no generators, which meant that they would have to go back to no electricity.

It wasn't as if there wasn't lots of gas available. There were huge storage tanks under every one of the service stations in the city. Huge storage tanks that were filled up regularly, which meant that they were likely close to full when the electricity first went off. The problem was not a lack of gas, but how to access it.

A clatter of metal hitting metal filled the air. Jim glanced to the left of the station where David was helping the boys pass the time by teaching them how to play hacky sack. "What was that?" he called out.

"Just a manhole cover," replied Les, "a small one."

"A manhole? In the middle of a gas station? Let me see it." Jim began striding across the lot with Samuel and Frank close behind.

"There's three of them," said Caleb. "One with a yellow ring, one with a red one and one with a white one."

Jim smiled as he reached down and turned the handle of the lid ringed in yellow. This was the answer. They didn't have to use the pumps. They didn't need a password to turn them on. This is where the tanks were filled. "We can take it out in the same way it goes in."

As he lifted the lid off the opening, he saw a long yellow plastic card with diesel written on it. "This is the diesel tank. Check the other ones," he called out.

"This one says regular," said Samuel as he pulled up the white lid.

"Premium here." Frank responded holding the red cover aloft.

Each man looked down into the opening in front of them. "Padlocked," said Frank.

"Same here," said Samuel.

"Well I guess that means we are going to have to get a bolt cutter," said Jim, "and then figure out exactly how we are going to get the gas from down there into our trucks." "Would a hand pump work?"

"I suppose so. Probably need a long hose, but we could try that."

"So that means we need to go shopping. The Home Hardware is right across the road. Come on boys, you can help me carry the stuff back here."

Everyone was outside when Jim arrived back with the boys in tow, all carrying something in their hands.

"We got a rotary pump and a lever one," said Jim. "Thought we may as well take two, since there's more than one tank to drain; lots of hose, some clamps, a knife and some coloured tape so that we know which pump is used in which tank. Who's got the bolt cutters?" "Here they are," said Jacob. "They're heavy."

"Trust you lads to leave the heaviest load for the youngest," Samuel retorted.

"Dad, I wanted to. They didn't make me."

"Okay. Well hand them over and we'll see how they work." Samuel eased the bolt cutter down into the opening. With two snaps the padlock was cut and easily removed. He handed them on to Frank. "Your turn."

In no time at all, the hoses had been lowered into the tanks and the gas was gushing from the pumps into the jerry cans. A pattern soon developed. As one can was filled, the pumper picked it up and took it over to his truck to pour the gas into the tank. One of the others stepped forward and started pumping into an empty vessel. Impromptu teams developed and the men began to race against each other, one team working with the lever pump and the other with the rotary. Even the boys took their turns as the men cheered them on.

It was getting close to noon by the time the fuel indicator needle on all six trucks pointed to F and the collection of containers were back in the truck boxes, all filled to capacity. Although everyone was tired and sweaty from the exertion of running the pumps, the competition had put them all in a good mood. The rotary team was declared the winner of the race, but only by a short lead of about one quarter of a jerry can. Everyone ignored his protests when Gareth questioned whether this was a true win since not all the containers were the same size.

As the pumps were pulled up out of the tanks and stored inside the service station, and the generator was loaded by in Trevor's truck to be used elsewhere, Paul approached Jim.

"I think we need a vac truck."

"A vac truck? You mean like in 'vacuum'?"

"Yes. This went well today, but it's going to take a lot of effort to do it every time we run out of gas. A vac truck would make it easier."

"Like the ones they use when they clean out my septic tank? Eeeyew!!"

"Yes, but that is only one thing you can use them for. They use them for lots of different things in the oil field. Like sucking up the water they need for the rigs from lakes and streams."

"Well we can't put our gas into anything with water in it and I certainly wouldn't want to try to clean one out if it had been used for something like cleaning septic tanks."

"We wouldn't have to do that. We could pull a Samuel and get a new one from one of the oil field supply lots. Could even get two if we wanted. One for diesel, just in case we ever need it and one for gas. It would be a lot easier than running these pumps."

"That's an interesting idea. Are you driving with anyone today?"

"Yes, David."

"Well, why don't you two go and see what you can find. I have to get some of this gas back to the girls before the generator in the house runs out. I'm sure anything you signed up for last night can wait until tomorrow."

Everyone piled into a vehicle and headed out to complete the task that they had signed up for the night before. As Jim drove back to the farm, he felt one load slipping softly off his shoulders. Now they not only had electricity but also access to a good supply of fuel to keep it going. Life was beginning to feel just a little more normal.

25

They called themselves the harvesters. Every day they spent some time combing the city for things that might be needed in the future for their survival. Every evening they brought what they had gathered to the farm to be stored in the large plastic bins, safe from moisture and rodents. During the meeting they reported on what they had collected and either crossed off or added things to the survival list. It had started out with the generators as the number one item and a variety of food items that were considered the necessities of life by the group: flour, salt, sugar, oatmeal, coffee, tea, yeast and spices. As time passed, more and more items were added to the list: flashlights, toilet paper, batteries, tampons and so on. Harvesting had become a never-ending chore.

Lucy liked being a harvester. This morning she lay in her bed thinking about the task she had volunteered for at last night's meeting. Teresa's trip into the city to find larger clothes for her children had led to the realization that all clothes were going to wear out in time. Since jeans were the garment of choice for all of the adults, it was decided that it wouldn't hurt to gather up a few bins of jeans in a variety

of sizes. Lucy had already decided where she would go –
Marks Work Warehouse. She should be able to gather quite a
variety there. Maybe the boys would want to join her today.

Lucy stepped out onto the deck with her first cup of
coffee of the day in her hands. It looked like it was going to
be a beautiful day. A warm wind had blown in from the west
a couple of nights ago bringing with it the promise of spring.

She took a deep breath. A frown creased her forehead.
What was that odour? She sniffed the air again. Yuk! That's
terrible! As she quickly rushed back inside and slammed the
door shut, a memory flashed through her mind. It was from
her days in nursing school. It was the smell of death that had
almost overwhelmed her as she looked down on the body
she was expected to dissect. The reality of the situation hit
her. The wind was warming up the houses. The bodies of
the dead were beginning to thaw. And now that they were
thawing, they were also decomposing.

Lucy went back to the bedrooms to wake up Trevor, Bill
and Les. "We're going to have to leave," she said. "Pack up
what you want to take with you. We're not going to be able
to stay in the city any longer. The bodies are beginning to
decay. It's a gut-wrenching smell from one of them. There
are thousands here. We won't be able to breathe."

One by one the vehicles from the city began to arrive at
the farm, each with a story of the awful smell that had taken
over their homes. As the group gathered together in the back
yard, they were all very aware that there was no way there
was enough room for all of them to live on the farm.

There were now forty-three individuals in the group.
Twenty-two more people had been located in the city

through their search efforts, including three men who had been living on the streets for years and had been sleeping in the Co-op. Trevor had found them sitting the curb in front of the Towne Centre Mall one afternoon, sharing a bottle of wine. They told him that they had moved into the mall as it had everything they needed. Soft beds to sleep in as well as a large supply of 'duzhe dobre'. Trevor smiled when he heard that term, one he had heard often from his Ukrainian neighbours whenever they were talking about alcohol. The three men refused to move out to the farm, claiming that they were more comfortable in the mall than they had been for years.

The rest of the newcomers were thankful that they were no longer trying to survive on their own and were ready to pitch in with the rest of the group. The same was true for a family who had been heading to Grande Prairie from the west who had found their way into the farmyard led by the sign Samuel had placed out on the highway. All of them had continued to live in homes in Grande Prairie. Now this was out of the question.

It was Marisa who came up with a solution for alternate housing for the rest of the group. "Why don't we utilize some of the motor homes out on the highway to Edmonton. The RV dealerships are the same as the car lots. They are lined with recreational vehicles of all sizes. They are north of the city so should be free of the smell, as least for now. The sooner we do this, the better."

As everyone around the room nodded their heads in agreement, Trevor spoke up. "That's a great idea, Marisa, and it's one I actually have experience with. We won't have to walk in blind like we did at the service station. I had a crash course in buying and running an RV when my parents picked out theirs and got it ready for their trip to Arizona. I assume we plan to take the big ones if we are going to live in them. They run on diesel so we will have to take the vac truck with diesel with us. They also have very large batteries which aren't charged up until they are sold, so we will have to deal with that. It isn't a problem, though. They also all have built in generators. We can use the batteries in our vehicles to start the generators which will charge up the batteries for us. So, make sure we have some booster cables with us. Other than that, this shouldn't be a problem, as long as we can access the keys."

"Wow," said Samuel. "Now this is harvesting to the extreme!"

"And if push comes to shove," said Alan, one of the new arrivals on the farm, "I can start any vehicle I need to with a screw driver."

"Sorry to throw a wet blanket on the party," said Jim thoughtfully. "If the bodies are decaying, we have to take care of Peter and Mary. Their house is directly west of us, which means we might not get the smell from the city here, but we will still get in from them. They wanted to die in their own bed together, and I let them. But they're still there."

"Has the ground thawed enough to dig a grave?"

"In certain places, I think. Those facing south, especially on a slope."

"How about her flower garden, Jim?" Frank's voice was soft and strained.

"That would work," Jim said thoughtfully. "And I think she would like to be put there."

"One grave for the two of them?'

"Yes."

"And we can use a tractor to dig?"

"Yes, Peter has a small one that he used for small jobs around the place after we took over the rest of the land. It's got a bucket on it. I'm sure it would do."

"Okay, then that's decided," said Stan. "The next question is whether we all stay here and deal with Peter and Mary as a group, or if we split up and some of us get the motor homes while those who don't need one stay here.

"Let's all stay here and have funeral," Margret said softly. "It will be a funeral for Peter and Mary, but it will also be a funeral for everyone else we have lost over the past weeks. I came up here to organize a funeral for my grandmother and we never had it because of the outbreak. I'd like to say good- bye to her."

"And Daddy" murmured Joelle. He's not going to come no matter how much we want him to."

"My mother," whispered Lily. "She was in a nursing home and they gave all of them the vaccination on the first day. I don't know who was looking after her as she lay dying. All of the staff were vaccinated first, so they would be too sick. I couldn't go to her. I had to protect the children." She began to sob quietly.

"Thank you, Margret," said Frank. "We never got to say good bye to Julie." He stood up and walked behind Jim and squeezed his shoulders as tears began to flow down his face.

Lucy started crying too. "We all lost so many, not only here, but all over the world. I'm thinking of my family back in Ontario." She reached for a tissue to wipe the tears from her eyes.

"We can write out all the names of those we lost on sheets of paper and put them into the grave with Peter and Mary. In that way it can become a resting spot for all of them."

"There's a large metal cookie tin in the pantry. You know the kind you get from Costco. Could we use that to put the papers with the names on, Jim?"

"Certainly." He reached up to squeeze Frank's hand, gave a deep sigh and rose to his feet. "Well let's get at it. Can someone bring the vac truck with gas across the road? I think that's what we will need for Pete's tractor."

26

May arrived in the midst of clouds and rain. Life in the community had fallen into a regular pattern, with everyone heading out to complete the assignment that they had chosen the night before to ensure their survival as a community. They returned to the farm for a communal supper, which had been cooked by whoever volunteered to take on that chore for the day. After the meal was finished, everyone gathered in either the back yard or in the living room depending on the weather. The list of priorities was updated on a daily basis, checking off what had been accomplished and what more needed to be done.

Everything had shifted in the last week of April as the temperatures soared and the homes in the city began to warm up. A convoy of motor homes arrived at the farm the day after the funeral, one for each of the families. A decision had been made, after much discussion, to park them in a long line next to the dugout on south edge of the small pasture.

"Dad always hated that dugout," Jim explained. "They put it there when they were building the highway. He didn't have any say whether he wanted it or not. We can use it to drain the sewage from the motor homes for now. We're going to have to do some research on how to make it not smell to high heaven, but I'm sure we can figure that out."

Harvesting had changed too. No longer were the harvesters going into the city to glean for the future. They were now heading north, south and west to the neighbouring farms and small towns, steering clear of anywhere that wreaked with decay. This had resulted in an increase of livestock on the farm. All of them were surprised at how many animals had managed to survive the winter without any care from humans. Pigs, ducks, sheep and another jersey cow had been hauled back to the farm by the harvesters. Those who volunteered for carpentry were kept busy building pens and sheds to house the livestock. Once it was determined that there were enough animals for the group, the harvesters changed their strategy. Fences were torn down; gates left open and barb wire was cut to allow the remaining animals the freedom to roam.

Margret and Frank were on their way into Grande Prairie. Discussion the night before had focused on the need to plant a garden to provide fresh vegetables. The major point of discussion was where they would be able to locate the seeds.

"I always get my seeds at Canadian Tire," said Lucy. "The few things I plant, that is. But they don't usually put their seeds out until March and everything closed down in early February.

"Same here," Teresa responded. Canadian Tire for me, too. Maybe we should check out the back of the store. They may have already arrived but not been put out on display.

Of course, the question is whether we can actually breathe if we go into the city. That's the only place we have access to a Canadian Tire."

"The smaller towns must also have seeds available somewhere. All of us can look for them wherever we are."

"This is definitely a priority isn't it?" said Jim as he began writing it on the list. Should I put everyone in charge of this?"

"We will have to scoop up everything we can find," said Samuel. They won't go bad if we keep them dry; and, this is something we are going to need every year, not just this spring."

Margret sat in the rocking chair by the fireplace, enjoying the heat and feeling no urgency to take part in this discussion. She had no idea where anyone would buy seeds back home in Minneapolis, much less here in Grande Prairie. As she rocked the faint memory of a parcel drifted through her mind. Katie had delivered a parcel for her grandmother. Was the label on that parcel McKenzie Seeds? It would make sense. Her grandmother had always loved gardening and had always spent the first few weeks after Christmas going through the seed catalogues, picking out and ordering what she wanted for the spring planting. Although she hadn't been able to do much of the actual gardening in own her yard for several years, she had taken to hiring young couples from the church to do the heavy work and sharing the bounty with them and others throughout the summer and fall. She had also taken a keen interest in the community garden and would order enough seeds for those who wished to be part of that activity but couldn't afford to buy the seeds themselves.

If Margret's memory served her well, there should be plenty of seeds for their garden in that parcel.

Finding seeds was not the only item on the agenda that Margret had for this trip. She had another major concern on her mind, which is why she had asked Frank to accompany her. He was the only person she felt safe enough to confide in.

Although she had been rehearsing what she wanted to say to him all night, she still didn't feel like she knew how to approach the subject. She finally decided to just blurt it out. "Frank, I think I have a problem."

"Yes, what is it?" Frank kept his eyes on the road.

"I think I am pregnant. It's either that or early menopause."

"And it's not John's, is it?' He paused for a few seconds and then completed the sentence. "Which is what makes it a problem."

"Yes," she said with a sigh. "Exactly."

"And you want my help to dispose of it?"

"Oh no, nothing like that. I just need someone to stand by me and help me figure out how to tell the girls. I've already got enough guilt about this without piling on more"

"I see. I suppose it's best not to tell them the whole story."

"I don't want to. But I know they're smart enough to figure out that it's not their father's so I will have to tell them something."

"You could claim that you were raped."

"I've been thinking of that, but it wouldn't be fair to the child, would it, to have stories like that circulating even before it is born? I just wish I hadn't left the house that day."

"Consequences!" It was Franks turn to smile at Margret as he said it. He turned his eyes back to the road. "Well, first things first. I'll give you a check-up and make sure that your suspicions are accurate and then we'll go from there. No use rushing into things if we don't have to."

"Thank you. I don't know what I would do without you."

"The same goes of me. I don't know what I would have done if Jim and I were the only ones left alive here. I'm guessing we would have decided to drive further afield to find survivors. Having the group gives us something to live for."

There was a lull in the conversation as they both thought about the possibility of going through everything they were experiencing without the support of each other.

Margret finally broke the silence as they neared the outskirts of the city. "I hope that it doesn't smell too bad."

"Well, it's been a few weeks now and there's no wind today so the stench should stay by the bodies."

"At least we know for certain that no one died in Grandma's house."

As they pulled up in front of her childhood home Margret felt the familiar pang of sorrow, knowing that her grandmother was no longer there to greet her. She got out of the car and stood looking at the house for a few minutes trying to adjust herself again to her loss. At least it seems that Frank was right about the smell, Margret thought, as she caught a faint whiff in the air. It's not too bad today.

The sign that Jim had taped to the door to tell John where they were was still there, though looking a little tattered and worn. Margret reached up with a sigh and pulled it free as she opened the door. We're not going to need this anymore, she thought, stuffing it into her coat pocket.

The parcel was lying exactly where she had placed it when Katie had delivered it so many weeks before. As she picked it up, she thought back of how she had shared coffee with her high school friend that morning. It was hard for her to believe that she was the same woman who had sat here drinking coffee with Katie. So much had changed. She felt like a completely different person. It was only three months ago but it felt like a lifetime.

Margret was also right about the label on the parcel. It did say McKenzie Seeds on it. She opened it up and looked through the seed packets. "There's everything we need here for a garden Frank," she said, "except potatoes. I think there may be a few of them left down in the basement. We had better take those too. It looks like there's lots of seeds, enough to supply vegetables for all of us, not only for this summer but throughout the winter if we do things right."

As Margret left the house she looked up at the sky and murmured, "Thank you Grandma." She knew perfectly well that her grandmother had not placed this order for the group. In fact, the seeds were a better indication that Grandma had no intention of dying. She was looking forward to another spring and summer. However, Margret didn't want to look at it that way in the moment. After all, it felt so much better to believe she was being looked after.

When they returned to the farm, they found Adam unloading a large rototiller from his truck. "I bought this last fall when they went on sale, with plans to start a large vegetable garden on our acreage. Last night I decided that it likely would make more sense to use it here. What do you think?"

"It's beautiful," said Margret, "and big. I've never seen one quite that large before. I have a feeling it would probably run away on me if I tried to use it. It sure will help with the garden though."

"I hope so."

Adam and his wife, Connie, lived on an acreage on the east side of Grande Prairie. She was a schoolteacher, who had come down with bronchitis shortly before the virus outbreak, so she was on sick leave at the time. Her doctor had advised her not to get the vaccination until the bronchitis had cleared. Her family had chosen to wait with her, and thus survived.

Samuel came across the Reese family while they were looking for food in the city and had invited them out to the farm. They had spent an enjoyable evening getting to know everyone but had decided they preferred to stay on their own acreage. The next evening, they arrived back on the farm. Their children Bradley, Jennifer and Penny had insisted that they join up with the group. They were tired of not having any other young people to interact with. Although they began actively working with the group, the Reese family continued to live on their own acreage until the bodies in Grande Prairie began to thaw and decompose. Since their acreage got the worst of the smell, they took up residence with everyone else in an RV on the farm.

Adam was a carpenter and his knowledge had proved to be very useful in the designing and building of the sheds and pens for the livestock that were being brought from nearby farms. He had recently become interested in solar energy; and, although he claimed he was only just learning, he began to introduce these concepts to the others. He was proving to be as good at teaching as his wife was, and he shared his talents and knowledge with the group.

Margret opened the package she was carrying, to show Adam the seeds her grandmother had ordered.

"Wow," he said. "This looks like it may be all we need this year. It's a pretty good haul!"

Margret smiled. "One thing about my grandmother, she never did do anything in a small way."

Frank joined in. "We can certainly be thankful for that and for you to Margret, for remembering this parcel existed."

27

Stan dashed up the steps of the porch and into the kitchen screaming, "The gun! Give me the gun!"

The women were sitting around the table having their last cup of coffee before heading out. They turned and looked at him in unison, all asking, "The gun?" They looked at each other. "We don't have a gun, do we?"

Stan shouted, "We've got to have a gun. There's a wild boar out there. You know how dangerous they are. I've got to kill him before he kills us. Didn't you watch those television shows?"

Teresa pushed her chair back and headed out to the porch with Stan right behind her. She looked out towards the pig pen where a black Hampshire boar with the tell-tale white shawl over its shoulders was nuzzling the nose of one of their sows through the fence. She turned to face Stan. "I have no idea what tomfoolery you were watching on TV, but there are a few things you don't seem to understand. First of all; we live in northern Alberta where we do not have wild boars terrorizing the countryside. Secondly, even if we do, that is a tame boar, one who was well cared for by a farmer until this winter and has no intention of killing you or anyone else. I can assure you that his tusks were cut off when he was just a piglet. That's what we farmers do, you know. And he is far more interested in sharing a little sex with our sows than anything else right now. If you'll get out of my way, we have a task to complete."

She opened the kitchen door and said, "Girls, can you come and help me. We need to put that boar in the pen so he can do his business. "Marisa, can you get a pail of grain? I'm sure we can entice him in with that."

Stan stayed on the porch watching as the women went out to the pigpen. Marisa climbed over the fence and poured the grain into the trough. Both sows rushed over and began eating. The women herded the boar around the pen to the gate. Teresa pulled it open and he too trotted over to the trough and began shovelling up the grain with his mouth.

Teresa returned to the porch, dusting off her hands. "See Stan, nothing to it."

Stan glared at her and went stomping off towards the line of motor homes. "Gareth," he called out. "Are you there, Gareth? You're coming with me."

Gareth appeared in the doorway of the motor home he was sharing with Paul. "What's up?"

"Come along. We've got some important harvesting to do." Stan turned and strode over to his truck, got in and slammed the door. "Those women think they can make a fool of me," he muttered. "We'll show them." As the motor roared to life, Gareth got in beside him. They spun out of the driveway in a rain of gravel.

The women stood on the front porch, watching them leave. "Well, that was interesting," said Lucy. She turned to Teresa. "I'm so glad you know so much about pigs. I wouldn't have known what to say to him. Or what to do, for that matter."

"When you're raised on a pig farm, it comes naturally. Pigs are pretty easy to work with if you treat them well." Teresa grinned and continued on. "We sure showed him, didn't we? Well let's go back in and finish our coffee, shall we? There's work to do."

The Fisher family were the last family to join the community. Frank had first noticed Stan's wife, Dottie, and their daughter, Becky, when he had seen them sneaking out of the back of a 7-11 convenience store on one of his trips looking for survivors in the south end of the city. He had watched them furtively creeping down the back alley and decided that it was not a good idea to approach them at that time. Instead, he noted the house that they entered. The next morning, he returned with Jim and Margret. They were prepared to be dealing with a woman and child. However, it was Stan who answered the door when they knocked and demanded," What do you want?"

Stan was a large man, with a booming voice and a perpetual scowl on his face. It appeared that he had watched every reality show that had ever been shown on television over the years. It was also apparent that he fully believed that he knew far more about survival than anyone else in the group because of this unique training.

He was constantly making one suggestion after another for improvements to the group, based on one episode or another of some type of survival reality series and ridiculing anyone who admitted that they had no idea what he was talking about. One by one they began to ignore him, hoping that this response would shut him up, but he appeared to be as oblivious to their rejection as he was to their bewilderment.

Stan had outright rejected the invitation that Frank, Jim and Margret had extended to the family at their door that morning. He claimed that they were doing quite well on their own and that they didn't need help from anyone. However, when the stench of death enveloped the city, it forced them out of their home. They had arrived on the farm along with everyone else and had become a part of the group.

Gareth ended up being the only person who was willing to spend any time with Stan. It appeared that Stan's focus on survival went along well with Gareth's conspiracy theories. Each evening they volunteered to be harvesters. Each evening they returned, usually choosing to bring back items that they felt were imperative for survival (in their own minds), rather than those that were on the priority list. The group stopped commenting on their decisions. It was far easier to keep the peace by letting them be than by arguing with them. Today wasn't any different.

"Hey Frank," Stan called out as they pulled into the yard that evening. "Come and see what we got."

As Frank approached the truck, the rest of the group gradually wandered over to see what was going on.

Stan grinned. "I think we got it all!"

"Got it all? What do you mean?" asked Frank.

"Every weapon we could find in the city. Plus, enough ammunition to last through anything that might happen." Stan paused and began to shake his head in disappointment. "I only wish we were living down in the States. Then we could have scored some major fire power! But this is the best we could do here with what's available. It should protect us."

"Protect us from what?"

"From anyone who wants to take over?"

"Take over what? The farm? Our homes? What?"

"Any of it. All of it. We need to protect ourselves!"

"We are the only people here. Are we protecting ourselves from each other?"

"No, of course not. From the gangs and the hoodlums and all that."

"And the government," interjected Gareth.

Stan went on as if he hadn't even heard Gareth. "We have to be prepared. Gareth and I spent all day gathering this together for everyone. You should be thanking us, not asking all these stupid questions."

Just then Jim drove into the yard. He got out of his truck and slowly walked over to the group gathered around Stan's Ford. "What the hell is this?" he said as he looked at the pile of guns in the back of the crew cab.

"Protection" Stan repeated. "We have to protect ourselves."

"No!" bellowed Jim. "No. No. No. No. No! We have been deciding everything by group consensus up until this point, and I am completely fine with that. But when it comes to this kind of stupidity, I say no. This is my land and you are not going to bring this kind of crap onto to it. You can store it anywhere you want, but I refuse to have it on my land. We are building a new world. We've spent too much time killing one another throughout history to go back and repeat it. Cooperation is the key to survival. We don't need these to cooperate with each other." He turned and began striding towards the house. "Get them out of here!"

Stan's eyes slowly circled the group, looking for someone who would support him. Everyone stared at him blankly, waiting to see what he would do. He turned and opened the door of his truck. "Well, I can see I'm not appreciated here. Gareth, get in the truck. Dottie, Becky," he hollered.

"We're leaving."

"But I don't want to leave," Becky whimpered. "I want to stay with my new friends."

"I know darling," Dottie said softly, "so do I, but we don't have choice. Come along now." With a bowed head she took Becky's hand and walked over to the crew cab. She opened the back door and lifted her daughter up inside. As she pulled herself up into the seat, Stan stepped on the gas and roared down the driveway. The truck door slammed as they went around the corner. It was the last they were to see any of them.

28

Margret and the girls were on their way to the Prairie Mall for a shopping trip. She had suggested it last night before the meeting, reminding them how Teresa had done this with her family before everyone had moved out to the farm. "I know it won't be the same as outings we took like this together when we were in Minneapolis," she said. "I'd like to spend some time with just the three of us. Do you mind?"

"Of course not, Mom. We'd love to do that." Joelle smiled at her mother as she spoke. Marisa nodded in agreement.

Marisa was at the wheel of her red mustang. She had celebrated her eighteenth birthday the week before. Samuel walked into the kitchen just as Margret was putting the finishing touches on the cake she was making for her.

He asked "what's up?"

She told him it was Marisa's birthday.

Sam replied "really," and headed out the door without another word.

That evening, during the meeting, Jim stood up and announced that they were celebrating a special birthday.

He'd gone on to thank Marisa for everything she had done for the group since they arrived on the farm, especially her willingness to share solutions to their problems. He'd finished his speech with the comment, "And now, in appreciation for everything you have contributed, we have a gift for you. Samuel stood up and handed her the keys to the mustang with a grin.

"Here you go, girl. We parked it behind the barn."

Today Marisa parked the mustang at entrance beside the grocery store, knowing that this had been harvested by the group in the past. They hoped they could get into the mall through this store but even if there was a door in the way, it would be one less to break open. Marisa was about to open the door of the mustang when Margret said, "No, please wait. I have something I need to tell you before we go in." She took a deep breath and began. "This isn't easy, but I want to tell you what is going on before you guess."

"Is this about you and Frank?" asked Marisa. "We have been noticing that you spend a lot of time alone with him."

"Oh no, nothing like that. Well yes, we have been spending time together but not because there is anything going on between us. He has been helping me."

"So what is it?" demanded Joelle.

Margret reached up and placed her hand over Joelle's as she held on to the seats in front of her. "Patience, my darling." She paused for a moment and then asked "do you remember the day that I went out into the storm?"

"How could we forget it?" cried Marisa. "We thought we'd lost you."

"I know. I am so sorry I caused you so much worry." She squeezed Joelle's hand under hers and then began speaking again. "Well, something happened to me that day and that's what Frank has been helping me with. First of all, when I got outside, I realized that I had grown up and I really had no interest in playing Storm like I did with Natalie when I was a child. But, it did feel good to be in the fresh air: and, I had put so much effort finding and getting into the winter clothes, I decided to explore a little. Everything was so still and quiet, except for the wind. It had a real spooky feel to it.

"I know what you mean!" exclaimed Joelle. "And that feeling has a name. I found it in a book I was reading. It's called 'kenopsia'. It's that eerie, forlorn atmosphere of a place that is usually bustling with people but now is abandoned and quiet."

"Wow, that explains it perfectly. Anyway, as I was walking down the street, I would look back at the smoke coming from the chimney and make that feeling go away thinking about you two. I was about to turn around and come home, when I saw smoke coming out of this other chimney and a path shovelled through the snow. It was at the Whites'. They were not only very good friends of my grandmother; but, they were also very good to me when I was a child. I got so excited! So, I went up and knocked on the door, but they weren't there. Another man was there. He told me that he didn't know who the Whites were or where they were. He needed somewhere to live that had heat, and had found that this house had a wood heater. No one was living in it, so he had moved in. I don't know much about him. I didn't even get his name. He was just a young man. He said he had come from New Brunswick to work in the oil field."

By now both girls were listening intently, while Margret was hoping that by not mentioning the store, the girls wouldn't accidently stumble on the real location. She certainly didn't want them to find his body. She took another deep breath and continued on. "He invited me in for tea. When I said no, he looked so despondent that I got worried. What if I left and he followed me back to the house? I didn't want that to happen. I took off my parka and my boots and joined him by the fire. It was okay in the beginning as we drank our tea and ate some biscuits that he found in the cupboard. But then, well: he forced himself on me."

"He raped you! Oh Mom, no!"

"And that's why you were so crazy after you got back to the house. I knew something bad had happened!" It was Marisa who was speaking now.

"Yes, and that's what Frank has been helping me with."

"But how did you get away?"

"Well, after that was done, he started talking crazy like. He called me Eve and claimed that we were married now because it says so in the Bible. He was ranting and raving that we were Adam and Eve and going to start a whole new human race together. That's why I took so long to come home. I didn't dare leave because I thought he would follow me. I needed to protect you. He finally fell asleep. I snuck out as quietly as I could. Thankfully the wind was still blowing so the snow was covering up my tracks as fast as I made them."

"And that's why you didn't want us to have a fire?"

"Yes."

"What happened to him? Why didn't the people who were looking for survivors find him?"

"That was my concern. I was so worried that he would appear on the farm every evening. I finally asked Frank to check the house for me. He was dead. It seems he killed himself. Being all alone so long seems to have driven him completely over the edge. I try to convince myself that I wasn't the final straw, appearing and then disappearing like that."

The girls had been shocked into silence. Margret pulled her hand away from Joelle's and turned to stare out the windshield. She bowed her head and clenched her fingers together. This was so hard.

"I didn't want to tell you any of this. I so wanted to spare you both, but I can't. You see there is another reason Frank is helping me." There was another long pause before she was able to blurt out the words. "I'm pregnant."

"Pregnant!" Marisa whispered as she turned to stare at her mother.

"You're going to have a baby?" cried Joelle.

"Or are you planning to have an abortion? I suppose Frank can help you that too. But then you wouldn't have to tell us, would you?"

"No abortion, Marisa. I am already carrying too much guilt about his death. I couldn't bear to take on anymore. And that's why I brought you here today. I want us to shop for baby clothes together before anyone else figures this out. Just us three. I hope you don't mind."

"Of course we don't mind Mom," Marisa replied. "We're here for you."

"A baby!" cried Joelle again. "I've always wanted a little brother or sister." She flung her arms around Margret's neck over the seat and buried her face into her hair.

"Grandma always said that we can never have too many people to love, and now I have to face that reality in a way I never dreamed I would. I am so glad I have you two beside me." Margret smiled at the girls and reached for the handle on the door. "Well, that's over. It's so good to have it out in the open. Let's go shopping. There's a specialty shop for babies in this mall. I thought we would check it out first."

They headed towards the mall, armed as usual with the crowbar, sledge hammer and bolt cutters that accompanied each of them when they planned to enter a building in the city that they hadn't been in before. This time they also carried large flashlights as they were aware that the mall had very few windows to let in the daylight.

Someone had been there before them. The door from the grocery store to the main hallway stood open, negating the need for the tools they were carrying. However, they knew that this didn't mean they wouldn't need them when they got to the baby shop. They were pretty sure that baby clothes hadn't ever been on the priority list. That shop would be locked up tight.

An uneasy hush fell over the trio as they entered the main mall. Spread out before them was the solemn reminder of the effort that the community had made to protect themselves from the virus. Tables and chairs still lined the hallways on both sides. Papers with a large number on it were still taped to each table. Waste baskets behind each table were piled to the top with disposable syringes and empty vials.

"Kenopsia," whispered Joelle.

"Yes, definitely 'kenopsia'. It kind of sends shivers down one's back doesn't it?" said Margret.

"Or it makes you want to cry," said Marisa.

"Yes, that too."

They switched on their flashlights as they rounded the corner, moving away from the daylight that was coming in through the entrance doors.

"Here it is," said Marisa. "Thankfully it has a glass door, not like that metal one that rolls down like we just passed. I have no idea of how anyone would get in there." She raised the sledge hammer into the air and propelled it through the glass.

"I remember the first time I did this when Samuel and I got his truck. I was so terrified that someone would come out and arrest us. It's so different now. Like it's the normal thing to do. Be careful of the glass." She stepped aside to lay down the hammer, allowing Margret and Joelle to enter first.

"So, what do we want? A boy or a girl?" asked Joelle as she swept the light across the row of tiny garments hanging on the rack against the wall.

"I don't think there is any way to tell," Margret responded. "I suppose we should get some of both. Aren't they adorable? And so soft." She raised a tiny sweater and rubbed it against her cheek.

The silence was broken by the shrill ring of a telephone. They stared at each other in shock. "There's someone here," whispered Joelle."

"No, not 'someone' Jo, 'something'. There's a working telephone here. How can that be? Where is it coming from?" Marisa dashed back into the hallway, looking wildly in all directions.

The phone rang again from behind a rolled metal door. "Here it is." She put her ear up against the door on the shop next to the one with baby clothes. "Now how are we going to get in there?" She grabbed the sledge hammer and hit the door with all the strength she could muster. It didn't move.

"I wouldn't be doing that if I were you. It's got to roll up and if you bend it, it won't move on the track. Can you see where they locked it? Maybe the bolt cutter will work."

"Nope."

The phone kept ringing.

"Blast it, with all the different shops in this place and different ways for us to get into them, the phone had to be behind this thing."

"Maybe there's a back door," said Margret thoughtfully. "As I remember, there's a hallway that goes back behind these shops and runs the whole length of this side of the mall. There's bathrooms back there too."

Marisa was already on the run. "Here it is" She dashed down the hallway and turned left. "Now let's see, that was the third shop from the hall so it should be this door." This time the power of the sledge hammer was effective. The door burst open. Marisa raced through the back of the shop through to the front counter and grabbed the handset. She gasped "Hello?" into the mouthpiece. No one answered.

"Hello?" she cried again, all the while trying to normalize her rate of breathing. "Hello?".

"There's no one there," she said, as Margret and Joelle entered the shop. Tears of disappointment filled her eyes. She was just about to drop the handset back into the cradle when she heard a soft male voice.

"Hello, who's there?"

"Hello, oh thank goodness you answered. We were so excited to hear the phone ring, and then it was so difficult to get to, and then there was no one there."

"Well, I'm here now. We're running an automatic calling system so we don't get to the calls as fast as if we were dialing in person."

"Who are you and where are you?"

"My name is John Abbot and I'm part of a group of students who are living in a university dorm in Seattle. We are all computer geeks, and we decided to see if we could reach anyone who had survived on a land line when we realized that the call centre for raising funds for the university was in the basement. One of our group insisted that they had discovered that the land lines kept working without electricity during the big tsunami in Japan. We didn't know if we should believe him, but we didn't think it would hurt to try. Now, who and where are you?"

"My name is Marisa and I am here with my mother, Margret, and my sister, Joelle. We came to the city to do some shopping and now we are in..." she shone the flashlight around the room, "in what appears to be a shoemaker's shop. We had to break the door down to get in here when the phone started ringing."

"So, you are on a land line then?"

"Yes, it appears so. It's one of those old phones you have to dial with your finger."

"Great. That means our assumption was right. The land lines are still open. And where exactly is this shoemakers shop?"

"It's in the Prairie Mall in Grande Prairie, Alberta, Canada. We are actually from Minneapolis, but we came up here because my great grandmother died, and we have been stuck here since. Everybody died, you see."

"Yes, most everybody died here too, it seems. We are only alive because we were so caught up developing a new app that we had no idea what was going on in the real world.

When we finally came to our senses, we discovered that we were the only ones left in the residence. Didn't have a clue what had happened until we read the newspapers that had piled up in the entry, and the notices posted on the bulletin boards advising students to return home. I guess the university decided to close down, once they realized the extent of the viral infection. Been staying put since then. Thankfully the dining hall had lots of food stored -- enough for the nine of us for a long time."

"There's only nine of you? There are forty-three of us in all. We are living on a farm on the west side of Grande Prairie. Most of the people died in their homes here after the big vaccination blitz. It was okay for a while, because the power went off and so all of the bodies froze. We had a very cold winter. When they started to thaw, they began to decay and the smell drove us out of the city. We are all working together, learning to survive. We harvest what we need from the city. Do you have electricity?"

"Yes, enough to get by on. The dorm has an emergency generator that is run through solar panels on the roof. It isn't as efficient as it could be, considering all the cloudy days we have in Seattle, but it does work. Once we turned off everything in the building we didn't need, it seems to keep up pretty good. And of course, we have the bikes."

"The bikes?"

"Yes, the bikes. Our parents were constantly nagging us about getting exercise, so we decided to buy some bikes.

The stationary kind you can ride and charge up your computer. An hour a day on the bike and we get 24 hours of power in our computers. They were happy when we told them we were riding the bike for an hour. They didn't realize, of course that it wasn't out in the streets or the parks like they imagined, but it kept them happy, so we didn't think they needed to know. Now, of course, we are pretty thankful we have them."

"Well, we're using gas-powered generators. In the winter we were relying on fireplaces and so on for heat and cooking. It wasn't easy. Once we got the generators hooked up and could use the appliances again, it was so much better."

"So, you go out into the community? We haven't tried that yet. Is it safe?"

"It appears to be. None of us who didn't have actual contact with the virus have gotten sick since we ventured out. There are a few with us who survived the flu by not going to sleep while they had it. Seems a little crazy, but it worked."

"That sounds fantastic! The rest of the gang are going to be so excited that we got through to someone. I can't wait to tell them. Do you know what number we called?"

"Oh, it should be here somewhere. Yes, 780- 555-9018. I think that's it. It's what's written on the business card. But we are going to take this phone back with us to the farm.

Hopefully one of the houses out there still has a landline working. If we don't find one that works there, we will come back here. In the meantime, is there a number we can reach you at?"

Margret handed her flashlight to Joelle, and carefully wrote the number on the back of the shoemaker's business card as Marisa repeated it to her. They said their goodbyes and promised to be in touch again soon. Marisa gently hung up the phone as she turned to stare at her mother. "Can you believe that? There are others alive! We have to go and tell the rest of the group."

"But first, let's take this with us." Margret picked up the thin cord and began tracing back to where it was plugged into the wall. She pulled if free, coiling it back to the set in her hand. She picked the set and headed towards the door. "I remember using this kind of phone when I was very little," she said. "I never imagined it could be the lifeline of the future."

Baby clothes were all forgotten as the women made their way out of the mall and headed down the bypass on their way back to the farm. "I'm so glad I got in there before it stopped ringing!"

"So am I. You moved pretty fast, if I must say so myself." Margret smiled at her daughter. "And now we know for certain that we aren't the only ones alive. There will be others. We just have to figure out how to connect with them."

29

Jim and Jack were on their way to the city. Jack had been a quiet member of the community until the meeting the night before, at which Marisa reported her conversation with John Abbot in Seattle. As everyone had begun to speak at once, in the excitement of finding out there were other people who had survived the virus, he joined the fray.

"Ham radio," he said.

No one noticed.

He pulled himself to his feet and repeated it in a louder voice.

"Ham radio."

Everyone turned to stare at him.

He sat down again and began to explain himself. "I used to be a ham radio operator. I have thought about it off and on since I moved out here. I didn't mention it because I didn't think there are many of us old fogies left who know how to run them. But now that we know there are other groups out there, I think we should get a ham radio. It's another way that we might be able to communicate with the world. I can teach anyone who is interested how to run it."

A buzz of excitement ran through the group. Jim offered to take Jack into the city to find a ham radio while others shared their interest in learning how to do it. The two men had started on their way as soon as they finished their breakfast.

As they drove east, Jack shared how he had first been introduced to the world of ham radio. His uncle was an avid operator from the time he was a teen. Whenever Jack visited his grandparents, Uncle Bob would take him up to his bedroom to show what he could do. Over the years he had built friendships throughout the world with different operators. He kept track of their locations with pins stuck into an old globe. As a small child, Jack was fascinated by the globe and the contacts that it represented with people so far away from their small village.

Jack had used his first paycheque to purchase his own set and had become a keen member of the local ham radio club. He and Uncle Bob had attended various ham fests held throughout the province in which one club visited another. But then Caroline came along and then the children and everything changed. Although he would still turn on the set for a chat now and then, it was no longer the main interest in his life. However, he had never forgotten the thrill of speaking with someone on the other side of the world. He paused his story and stared out of the window, lost in the memories of his youth.

Jim took this opportunity to ask, "So Jack, where are we going?"

Startled, Jack glanced at Jim and asked, "What did you say?"

Jim repeated his question. "I'm not sure. It's been a number of years since I was involved with the ham radio. When my hearing started to go, I completely lost interest and then Caroline donated all my equipment to the church for their annual flea market. She was that kind of a woman. Kept the house spic and span and got rid of anything that might be collecting dust. I didn't argue at that point, but once I got my hearing aids I wished I had stood up for myself and kept it. It was too late."

"So, we're not going to your house then. Where would we find a new one?

"Well that's my problem. It's not a big item for stores, you see. Only a limited number of people are involved in this, so even back when I got my equipment, I had to order it through a catalogue. Nowadays, I expect most people depended on the internet."

"That's out of the question."

"I know, and that's the problem. I guess we might try Radio Shack or something like that."

"Isn't that the one that changed its name to The Source, or sold out to them, or something?"

"Not sure. At my age one doesn't keep up on things like that."

"Well there's a Source on the way into town. We'll try that first."

As they entered the store, Jack gazed around with a confused expression. "Oh dear, I haven't got a clue what any of this may be used for."

Well, you're the only one who is going to be useful here. I don't even know what we are looking for." They switched on their flashlights as they moved towards the interior of the shop.

"I guess it's best to read the boxes on the shelves. By the way, ham radio is the common name but they may also be called wireless or citizens band radio. He began to walk slowly down the aisle shining his flashlight on the boxes stacked on the shelves. Jim followed suit scanning everything on the other side of the store. When they met at the back they both shook their heads.

"I can't see anything at all with any of those words on it. You?"

"No."

Jim raised his head, skimming the shelves that were filled to capacity, with his eyes. "So much stuff. So worthless to us right now That's what was happening with this new generation. Technology was moving along so fast that everything was based on making it obsolete without anyone thinking of the long-term consequences. What a waste!"

"New generation, hey. That's what we have here. So why don't we go 'old'? Why don't we try the antique stores?"

A deep sense of disappointment engulfed Jim and Jack as they arrived back at the farm that afternoon. They had spent the whole day searching the city for a ham radio without any luck. "It seemed like a good idea," said Jack in a desolate voice. "But I guess it's a thing of the past. No good to us today."

"But it isn't," Les responded eagerly as he entered the room. "I was reading about it in the newspaper in January, just after we had finished our exams. I was looking for something to do outside of school, and classes were being offered by the Northern Alberta Radio Club, or something like that. There was an advertisement in the paper and also an interview with a fellow they said was the local representative of the club. If we can figure out who he was and where he lived, we should be able to find his set. I'm pretty sure that I kept a copy of that paper. I was still considering it as a possibility. I didn't know that I would end up with a teacher right here."

The next morning there were three in the truck heading into the city. First, they stopped at the James home where Les ran up to his bedroom in hopes that the paper was still there. It was. Their second task was to find a phone book, hoping that this man had been living in his home for a number of years. The phone companies had stopped printing phone books when cell phones had taken over. There wasn't one in the James' home, so they headed over to Margret's grandmother's house. Marisa was sure she had seen one there. They scored again.

Step three was to find his address in the phone book. Les crossed his fingers as they went through the pages. Yes, here it was. At least it was the same name. It was possible that there could be more than one person with the name. There was only one in the phone book. Hopefully it was the man they were looking for.

Fred Peters lived in a small bungalow on the south side of the city. It was a neat home with cedars standing at attention on each side of the steps leading up to the front door. They approached slowly, with a slight feeling of dread as they knew there were likely bodies inside. This was the first time any of them had ventured into a home of the dead.

Habit had them knocking on the door and patiently waiting for a response that they didn't expect to get. Jim was about to raise the sledge hammer to break the lock, when Jack reached for the door handle. It turned and the door slid open. They looked at each other uneasily.

"I wonder how many people left their doors unlocked when they were sick, in hope that someone would come in and help them?" said Jim.

"Probably a lot," said Jack. "I know I did that last week before you found me. Didn't want to have them break down the door when they came to bury me. It likely was the same for most everyone."

"It's so sad." Lester's voice trembled. "Do you really think we should be doing this?"

"If it's the only way we can get a ham radio, then we have to. I'm sure he'd be happy to know his equipment was being used. I know I would if I was in his shoes."

The wrank smell of decay washed over them as they stood in the doorway talking.

"Eeeyew!" Lester reached up and pinched his nose closed. "He's in here all right. We had better get moving. We don't want to stay in here too long."

Jim headed towards the back of the house. "I'll open the back door in hopes we can get a breeze through to decrease the smell. You two find the radio."

They began exploring the house on tiptoes, softly closing the bedroom doors where they could see the form of a body lying on the beds. There was nothing on the main floor, so they extended their search to the basement. There they found a study with the radio equipment set up on a desk.

"Here it is!" cried Jack with a delighted look on his face.

"Everything we need." He picked up a notebook and glanced through it. "Just as I thought. Here's his call letters and the other people he was in contact with. We should take everything. There's probably an antenna outside too. We'll need that."

Life on the farm had become much easier as May moved into June. The garden had been planted and the seedlings were beginning to push their heads up above the ground. Weeding and watering the garden were now high on the priority list and everyone was expected to do his or her part. This meant that the sense of boredom and futility, so common when trying to keep the ground clear of weeds, was almost nonexistent because the job was spread out amongst them all.

As the plants began to grow, the sense of urgency that had plagued everyone for the last few months seemed to dissipate. Although the nightly meetings continued; and, the priority list was kept up to date, the feeling that one needed to be constantly busy was gone. It all started with a discussion around the wisdom of planting crops. Although it felt like the logical thing to do, the final consensus was that there was already so much grain available in the steel granaries on the farm and on other farms in the vicinity, that there was no need to go to that effort.

In the meantime, the hay was almost fully grown. Most of the men were getting the mowers, rakes and big round baler ready to provide the winter feed for Julie's herd. Samuel drove out to his farm in Albright to pick up his square baler, as the smaller bales were much easier to work with for the milk cows and the sheep.

Jim arrived in the kitchen one afternoon with an armload of red rhubarb stalks. "Does anyone know how to make use of these?" he asked. "Mary had several plants out in her garden, and I decided to check on them today to see how they were doing."

The first fresh fruit of the season had arrived. Teresa and Lucy immediately set to work making rhubarb crisp for the evening meal. Everyone oohed and awed over their desert and the decision was made to harvest as much of this as possible while it was at its highest quality. "There's nothing quite a delicious as food straight from the garden," said Lily.

The next few days were spent combing the back yards in the city, gathering up as much rhubarb as possible. A surge excitement of being able to preserve food for the coming winter filled the air. The kitchen was busy with women bottling rhubarb jam and relish for the winter, as well as cutting up the stalks into one-inch pieces and bagging them for the freezer. In the meantime, others showed off their culinary skills. Marisa and Joelle surprised everyone with rhubarb muffins for breakfast one morning, and Frank spent a day in the kitchen sharing the rhubarb cream pie that was a special treat in his family.

The days were getting longer. Meetings now took place around the fire pit in the backyard, with everyone comfortably seated in the large variety of lawn chairs and lounges that the men had salvaged from the Home Hardware. The discussion of the evening focused on how to find locations where the group could harvest other fruits of the summer when Sam and his sons entered the yard carrying an assortment of fishing rods and nets. The conversation paused as everyone looked up to welcome them.

"I'm sorry we're late," said Sam. It took a lot longer than we expected to come up with enough of this for all of us, but we managed. Yesterday morning, Jacob woke me up with a question. He wanted to know if we were going to the fishing derby for Father's Day. It's been something that we have done for the last few years and we really enjoyed it. I told him no, I was sorry, but there wasn't going to be a fishing derby this year. There was no one left to organize it.

"However, I couldn't get it out of my mind all day yesterday. This morning, when I woke up, I said to myself, 'Why don't we have our own fishing derby?' So today me and the boys have been collecting all the gear we need. If everyone is agreeable, I suggest we pull together a picnic lunch for tomorrow and drive up to Spring Lake for a day of fishing. It's Father's Day and I personally think we can afford to take the time off. Of course, if you don't want to do this, my family is going to do it anyway, just for old time's sake."

"Sounds like a great idea to me," said Paul. I'm definitely in."

"Us too," said Adam as he gestured towards his family. "Unless, of course, you have something else planned for me, Connie?"

"Nothing more than breakfast in bed, but we can still do that. This sounds like fun.

One by one each family voiced their agreement.

"You say you've got enough equipment for all of us?" asked Jim.

"Yep, everything I could think of. Rods, reels, line, nets, hooks, flies, even some filleting knives and a cooler to keep what we catch cold. We cleaned out every sports store and sports department in the city when it comes to fishing gear."

Summer fruit was forgotten as everyone began to make suggestions for the next day. "Why don't we take enough food for a couple of meals and spend the whole day there? The days are getting so much longer; and, it's not like we have a definite schedule to meet tomorrow, other than looking after the livestock."

"We've got a canoe at home," added Bill. "We could pick that up and bring it with us."

"We used up all of the potatoes in the garden, but I could make a pasta salad."

"And we've got lots of eggs. I can boil them up for deviled eggs if people would enjoy them."

"Pete had a small boat. I'm sure it's still in the garage on a trailer. I can hook it up and take it along."

"How about a wiener roast for lunch and a fish fry for supper? I think that there are still cases of wieners in the freezer downstairs that we moved here from Save On Foods."

"We can stop in Beaverlodge on the way and see what kind of snack foods we can pick up. We don't keep too much of that stuff around here but it might be nice to have them as a treat for a change."

Margret stood up, her eyes shining. "Spring Lake! It's been years since I've been there. Grandma had friends near there, and we would often go out to Valhalla for church services on Sunday and then spend the rest of the day at Spring Lake. It's such a relaxing spot. But it's getting late. I think I'll head off for my beauty sleep so I'm ready to help in the morning."

31

Sundays became days of rest and relaxation on the farm. Father's Day at the lake had turned out to be a wonderful idea. The day in the sun away from the farm, combined with the competition as each person tried to reel in the biggest fish, reminded them all of how much just having fun added to their lives. Meetings on Saturday nights now focused on how to enjoy themselves on the next day. Games and sports equipment of all kinds were harvested along with food and other necessities. The children were absolutely delighted with this turn of events.

Marisa and Paul headed into the large pasture with the children at their heels. They had volunteered to organize a soft ball game for children the night before. The pasture gave them plenty of room to set up the bases. Samuel's dog Buck loped on ahead of them. Suddenly he stopped and began to growl. His body stiffened and the hairs on his shoulders stood up as the growl deepened.

"What's wrong Buck?" Marisa asked. She turned to Paul. "I've never seen him acting like this before, have you? "

"No, I haven't" Paul answered. He turned and put his hand up to stop the children who were following them. "Sssssh! Something's up."

Together they scanned the area that Buck was staring at. "Do you see anything?"

"No. Wait – yes, there is something black moving over there behind the pig pen. I can't quite make out what it is."

"It looks like a bear, said Caleb. "We had one in our yard a couple of years ago. "

"You're probably right, Caleb." Paul responded. "Marisa, you and Caleb take the children back to the RV's and have them all go inside. I'll get Jim."

"Come on kids. Quietly now. We don't want anyone to get hurt. Caleb, can you bring Buck?"

By the time that Paul reached the farmhouse, all of the children were inside their homes, peering out the front windows along with their parents. He found Jim seated at the table in the kitchen, reading an old magazine.

"Hey Jim, sorry to disturb your Sunday rest, but we need to talk to you. We've got a problem out there."

"What's up?"

"Well, we know your opinion on having guns on the farm and...."

"My opinion on guns? What do you mean?"

"Well, how you don't want to have any guns on the farm."

"I've got guns."

"You have?"

"Yes, of course I have. Every farmer has guns. I have a rifle, a shotgun and a twenty-two. They're locked up in the back of my closet with the ammunition."

"But what about your reaction to Stan?"

"Stan brought those guns here to kill people. My guns are not for that. They are used for hunting and for our animals here on the farm, when needed. They would never be used against people. It's a direct contrast to Stan's purpose. Of course, there are no longer any people for Stan to use his guns on, but he never thought of that. He was so stuck in his belief that everyone is out to get him, that he needed to protect himself with force, it was terrifying. So guns aren't the problem. What is?"

"There is a big black bear nosing around the back of the pig pen. It's just a little too close for us to be comfortable. We were going to play softball in the pasture when we noticed it."

"That's not good. Bears usually don't come close to our homes unless there is a problem of some kind or another. They shouldn't be hungry at this time of the year, especially with the different livestock out there, on the loose. I wonder if it's been injured in some way."

"We didn't get close enough to see anything. Marisa took all the children back to the RV's so they would be safe. I do have my hunting rifle in my RV, but I didn't want to pull it out without your permission."

"Well, you certainly don't need my permission, but I do appreciate the thought. How many of the group thought the same thing as you?"

"All of us, I expect."

"Okay. If you know of any others with rifles, let them know. I'll get mine and you go and get yours. We'll meet up behind the barn."

In no time at all the men were staring down at the carcass of a large male black bear at their feet. A thin wire was wound around his front right front leg, cutting deep into his flesh. Thick puss oozed out of the cut.

"Look at that wire. I wonder where he picked that up. It almost looks like a snare of some sort."

"It's been on him for a while, considering how deep into his leg it is and how extreme the infection is. I wonder how he could even walk on it. Must have been terribly painful."

"It's too bad that we had to shoot him, but there are too many little children here to take any chances. I don't know if there was any other way to help him."

"I don't know much about bears, but I doubt he would last long with an infection like that," said Frank. Terribly thin, too. I expect we put him out of his misery."

"I've heard that bear fat is good for many things that ail you. Should we attempt to harvest some?"

"By the looks of him, the fat is long gone. Better just to bury him, if you ask me."

And so, they did.

Jim started off the meeting that evening with an apology to everyone for giving them the wrong idea about his opinion on guns. "I never dreamed that you would take my reaction to what Stan and Gareth had collected, as proof that I was one hundred per cent against guns. But I suppose it kind of makes sense when you think of how extreme I was. I'm sorry about that. I was just trying to protect everyone."

"We appreciate that" said Samuel. "But we were also aware that something like this might happen and we wanted to be prepared. We apologize for not saying anything to you."

"No harm done. Anyway, let's get it all out the open. How many guns do we actually have here? Where are they and how are they being stored? My main concern is that we make sure that we keep them out of the hands of the children."

32

Margret was in the kitchen preparing spaghetti sauce, using the last of the tins of tomatoes she had found in the back of the pantry. She lifted the spoon to her lips and sipped, looking out across the pasture as she savoured the flavor. She reached for a clean spoon and offered a taste to Teresa, who was sitting at the desk in the corner patiently dialing one phone number after another.

"What do you think?"

"Hmmm. A little more garlic perhaps?"

"Yes, that's what I was thinking. However, I love garlic and I want to make sure I don't overdo it. Having any luck?"

"No. This is our old address book and so there are phone numbers in here from all over the country. I was so hoping I would come up with something. It seems that everyone we knew removed their land lines when they got cell phones."

"All of us are hoping. That's what I found with Grandma's address book, too. I thought I might have some luck with her friends, as they were older. But nothing."

"It's so disappointing."

"The price of progress, I guess. Why waste money on a land line when you have a phone in your pocket?"

"Yes. I guess it made sense at the time. Oh well, I have a few pages left. I'll keep on trying."

With the arrival of the old telephone and the ham radio, a new task appeared on the priority list. It was called 'connecting with the outside world'. One could either sign up to learn how to operate the ham radio with Jack, or use the phone to dial the numbers they had for friends and family -- just in case they were still alive. Everyone had signed up for this task at one point or another.

Jim had been pleasantly surprised to hear the dial tone when they plugged the shoemaker's telephone into the phone jack in the wall. He hadn't remembered Julie disconnecting it at any point, but since they were both in the habit of using their cell phones, he also wasn't sure that it was still connected. He couldn't remember how long it was since he had actually talked on the house phone.

"So," he said, holding up the telephone that had been plugged in to the jack before, "why wasn't this one working?"

"As far as I understand," said Marisa," that one needs electricity to work and this one doesn't," as she pointed to the set on the desk.

"Ah, that makes sense. Julie unplugged it from the electrical outlet when we were getting too many calls from telemarketers. So, you're saying that it won't work at all if it needs electricity, or that it might if we have generator hooked up to this outlet and plug it in?"

"I'm not sure. I am certainly not the expert here. All that the guy in Seattle told me was that it had to be a landline. In the meantime, this one is working, so I'm going to use it."

"Well good luck. Don't get a sore finger dialing."

Marisa reached in her pocket and pulled out her cell phone. As she did so Jim asked, "What do you need that for?" in a puzzled tone.

"All my contacts are in here. I charged up the battery last night so I could get to them. Don't worry, I will still use my finger to dial."

By noon that day, Marisa was bored, tired and very disappointed. She had dialed everyone on her contact list without any response. Logically she knew that the majority, if not all of the numbers she was calling, were cell phones; but, deep in her heart she also felt she had to try. She so hoped that this phone would allow her to connect with someone back home in Minneapolis. In desperation she finally called the number of the dorm in Seattle. At least there should be someone there to talk to. Their phone rang and rang and rang, but there was no answer.

Lucy took over the phone after lunch. She had retrieved her address book from her house in the city that morning. It was one of those items she had thought she no longer had any use for. Her calls were all going to Ontario where the majority of her family lived. In the end, she had some success dialing a couple of numbers that actually rang on the other end; but again, no one answered, no matter how long she let the phone ring.

In the meantime, Jack had set up the ham radio in his bedroom. He was delighted to discover that the younger boys were fascinated with this equipment, and he was eager to teach them everything he knew. He explained each piece in detail, describing what it was used for. Once everything was set up, he explained the difference between making a call in the past and making one now. In the past one would slowly turn the dial until one found a frequency that was silent as one did not want to break into someone else's call. However, under their current circumstances, the goal was to actually find a frequency that was active. As he slowly turned the dial, he asked the boys to listen carefully to the trans receiver for any sign of life. They had heard nothing but static.

Margret turned away from the stove to face the door as footsteps thumped up the back-porch steps. It opened to reveal the lanky forms of Lester, Todd and Caleb.

"Good morning boys," said Margret.

"Good morning. Is Elmer upstairs?

"Elmer?"

"Yes, He promised to teach us how to send out messages on the radio this morning."

"You mean Jack, don't you? We don't have any Elmer living here."

"He wants us to call him Elmer. That's the handle for someone who teaches others how to operate the ham radio."

"Okay, then yes, he's upstairs as far I know. I haven't seen him this morning. Have you Teresa?"

Teresa looked up from the address book and replied, "No, not this morning. I don't even think he's been down for breakfast yet."

The boys headed towards the stairs as Margret called after them "See if he's hungry."

Silence descended on the kitchen for a few minutes. Margret lifted the spoon to her lips again. "I think it's perfect now. We'll let it simmer for a couple of hours. Are you ready for a break, Teresa? I can make some tea."

Her words were drowned out by the sound of Lester pounding down the stairs. His face was white as he burst into the kitchen. "You have to come upstairs. There is something very wrong with Jack."

As the three of them dashed up the stairs, Lester cried out, "He's sitting at his desk with his head down on his arms like he is sleeping. But we can't wake him up."

Jack was sitting at the desk as Lester had described, slumped over with his head on his arms as if he had decided to take a nap. Margret and Teresa gently raised his head.

"He's still warm and he seems to be breathing, but it is very shallow. Can you help us lift him into the bed?"

As they lifted him away from the desk a paper fell out of his hand. Todd reached down and picked it up. He read, " 'Hello CQ CQ CQ this is H14KUB Hawaii one four Kilo Umbrella Bravo calling CQ 20 meters and standing by for a call.' I don't know what this means. I guess it's what he was planning to teach us."

Margret looked at Teresa. "Do you have any idea where Frank is today? Or even Lucy?"

"No," said Teresa. "I don't. We could check the priority sheet."

"I'll get it!" Lester cried and rushed back down the stairs. It only took a minute for him to re-enter the room with the sheet clutched in his hand. "It looks like both Frank and Lucy were planning to go to the hospital today to harvest something. It doesn't say what."

"Can you go and get them, Teresa? I'll stay here and watch over Jack."

"We'll go with you," said Caleb. "That hospital is huge. We can find them faster if there are more of us."

"Hurry! Oh, and by the way. Please turn off the spaghetti sauce on your way out."

Margret pulled the chair away from the desk and set it close to side of the bed. She sat down and took Jack's hand in her own as she studied his face. He was so pale, and his breath was so weak, but he was still alive. She murmured softly, "Stay with us Jack. Frank and Lucy are on the way. They'll know what to do."

The minutes slipped by slowly. As Margret sat holding his hand, she realized that his breath was getting slower and slower. It finally faded away completely. His hand went limp in hers.

She stood up and began shouting into his face. "No. No. No. Wake up. Please wake up. They're almost here."

But it was no use. Jack was gone. Margret slumped back into the chair as tears began to run down her cheeks and sobs shock her body. So many, many losses. When would they stop? She wept for Jack and how his desire to help them with the ham radio had been thwarted. She wept for the goodbye she never got to say to her grandmother before she died. She wept for John, lost on the road somewhere and for her parents who hadn't been allowed to see her grow up. She wept for her house in Minneapolis. It was her perfect home, and she would never see it again. She wept for the vibrant city she had grown up in that now stood decaying and deserted. She wept for her friend Katie and the dinner that they had never had. She wept for her children, with all their plans for the future, which would never be realized. She wept for her baby, who would never know John or his biological father. She wept for the woman that she had been, waiting, always waiting for someone else to steer her life in the direction they wanted. She wept until she couldn't weep anymore.

As Frank walked into the room, he glanced at Jack's face. It told him all he needed to know. He silently walked over to Margret and tenderly picked her up in his arms. He carried her down the hall to the master bedroom where he laid her in the bed and wrapped the blankets around her. She immediately fell asleep and didn't wake up for the next twenty-four hours.

33

Margret sauntered through the farmyard slowly, taking the time to enjoy the fresh air and feel the sun on her face. She was heading towards the chicken coop to gather eggs. She knew she didn't have to hurry. She had time to relax while the rest of the women assembled the other ingredients. Marta had volunteered to teach anyone who was interested how to make pasta from scratch. One of the most important criteria, she insisted, was using the freshest eggs possible, right from the chicken. Margret was on her way to get those eggs.

Marta Mazur and Lena Nowak were two young women who had immigrated to Canada from Poland over a year ago. They both worked at the Prairie Rose Manor, a nursing home for seniors; and, had both been on their first vacation when the virus scare began. However, they had also taken on the position of co-managers of their apartment block and thus couldn't afford to leave the city for their holiday. Instead, they had chosen to stay put and enjoy the free time they had to explore their surroundings.

The first they knew of the virus was when their sponsors phoned to ask if they had received the vaccination. When they said no, they advised them to do so a soon as possible. However, a crisis in the apartment building erupted, as pipes broke in one of the upper suites, flooding the rooms below. Marta and Lena were stuck cleaning up the mess and waiting for the plumbers to come and repair the damage. By the time that was settled the vaccination blitz had been abandoned.

Their families in Poland had kept in touch via the internet and shared how the virus was running wild in their country. They advised them to stay indoors, away from anyone else who might have come in contact with the illness. They had done so, huddling together in the smallest room in their apartment, covered in blankets to keep warm throughout the coldest of the winter. They had rationed their food as best as they could, eating only a little each day. They had finally emerged from the building, weak and hungry a few days after the last of their food was gone. Samuel found them sitting together on the front steps, too weak to go any further.

A sudden movement to left caught Margret's eye as she walked along. She glanced up at the hayloft where a silhouette of a female form appeared in the doorway. What a perfect body, she thought and then gasped as she realized who it was. A young man's form appeared beside the woman. She opened her mouth to scream "Joelle," when a hand clamped itself over her mouth and an arm tightened around her mid-section, just above her bulging abdomen.

"Ssssh! It's okay," said a man's voice as he picked her up and carried her between the barn and the chicken house.

"Jim?" Margret tried to cry out, but the hand stayed in the way.

"Yes, it's me, Jim," said the voice. "I know what you saw. I know it upset you. I don't think you want to embarrass your daughter." He deposited her on the ground and eased his arm from around her body. "Are you going to scream?"

She shook her head no and leaned back against him as he let go of her mouth. "She's too young, Jim. She shouldn't be doing that with a man."

"Ssssh. I know. I know, but if you had watched any longer you would have realized it wasn't her first time and it's not going to be her last. It's inevitable."

"But she should be out with her friends, going to dances and movies and football games."

"All those things that don't exist in our world any longer."

"But they should. We shouldn't have lost them. Oh Jim," Margret turned and bent forward, crying with her head against his chest. "I just realized that I am treating this all like a vacation. That it's soon going to be all over and we can go back to the way we used to live."

"That would be nice, wouldn't it? But I'm afraid it's not possible."

"This is it, isn't it Jim? This is our life whether we want it or not."

"I'm afraid so."

"And here I am, blubbering all over your shirt. I'm sorry Jim. I'm such a fool."

"Not a fool, Margret. A strong, wise, desirable woman, stuck in a situation that you have little control of. Just like the rest of us."

"Desirable! Oh Jim, don't lie. I know what I look like."

"You're beautiful Margret. Absolutely beautiful, and if you want the truth, I am looking forward to doing just what those two young kids are doing up in the hayloft with you sometime. With your permission of course."

Margret gazed up at his face in shock.

"You know, I never thought there would be another woman in the world for me but Julie, but as I've been watching you throughout the months, how you pitch right in, and how you stick up for your daughters and how you are dealing with this pregnancy. Well, you got me. You're quite a woman. And in this new world, you are the woman I want by my side."

"But what about Frank?"

"Frank?"

"Well, the girls seem to think that if anyone is interested in me, it's Frank. Not that I want him. If you ask me, I'm too old for anyone. I just wouldn't want to cause any trouble."

"Well, you don't have to worry about Frank. As far as I understand, he's got his eye on Lily."

"Lily?"

"Yep, seems he has figured out that she knows far more about keeping the body healthy than he does, in spite of all his medical training. It fascinates him."

"So, you? Me?"

"Only if you want. I know I do."

"After the baby comes?"

"If that's what you want. Just don't forget, I'm here for you anytime you need me."

"Need you! Oh no! I'm supposed to be getting eggs for the pasta. The women are the ones that need me. Thank you, Jim. You've given me a lot to think about."

Margret hurried back to the kitchen with the pail of eggs, a smile tugging at the corners of her lips. Jim! Who would have thought?

34

Jim stood on the front verandah with his coffee cup in his hand watching the sun rise in the east, remembering how much Julie had enjoyed it each morning. He turned to Margret, who was standing beside him and remarked "Julie would have declared this a perfect start to a perfect day. I think I agree. It's going to be a wonderful day for a celebration."

"I do to" replied Margret. "I wish she could be here with us."

Alan and Lindsey Bergman were in the kitchen preparing the turkeys for the Thanksgiving feast. Like the Burdocks, they had reached the point of leaving their farm and driving towards Grande Prairie in hopes of finding food. They turned south when they saw Samuel's sign posted on the highway.

The Bergmans were the only family to arrive on the farm with livestock in their vehicle. Along with their four children: Tammy, Todd, Toby and Tommy, they had a crate with five turkeys in the back of their SUV, the last remaining members of their breeding flock. The rest were lost to the cold when the power went off.

Alan had brought four hens and one tom into their house, in order to salvage what they could. These large birds were added to the flock in the chicken house. Shortly after they arrived, they began the process of laying and hatching eggs. Today's meal would include four of the young toms that had grown up over the summer.

The Bergmans were strict adherents to the alternative health movement that had swept the world over the last few years. They refused to eat anything that was not organic or to plant any of their crops with GMO seeds. Their turkeys were all bred on their farm and raised free range during the summer. All but fifty were sold off each fall. The rest were pampered throughout the winter in a heated barn to repeat the process of rebuilding the flock each spring. Being free range meant that they never got as huge as most turkeys sold in the supermarkets, but they were far tastier and a popular choice for their customers.

Alan and Lindsey hadn't even considered getting the vaccination for themselves or their children. They couldn't see the logic of injecting a large number of poisons into their bodies along with viruses. They believed that the immune system they got at birth would do its job, as long as they provided the necessities of life: good food, clean water, exercise and lots of sleep. They believed that not exposing themselves to pathogens was far more effective than getting a vaccine and so they stayed home. The events of the year had supported their view.

Out in the yard, other members of the group were setting up a long line of tables made of sawhorses and sheets of plywood. King sized bed sheets were spread over the plywood to serve as tablecloths. Stacking lawn chairs were arranged down each side of the table, one for each member of the group. Each end was left empty, a decision that had been made the night before. It signified the reality that there was no one person in charge of the group. They were all equals.

Sarah, Rose, Penny and Jennifer had spent the past week making place cards for each member of the group. They placed them all in a bucket and were now pulling them out one by one to place in front of each chair, in an attempt to ensure that the seating plan was as random as possible. In the meantime, the older girls, Joelle, Susie, Marisa and Tammy were arranging bouquets of fall leaves and flowers for the centre of each section of the table.

As the garden flourished, group members began to concentrate their efforts on harvesting fruits to go with the vegetables they were growing. Some went into the city to search out the fruits trees that were growing in the backyards of many of the homes. Others made the effort of checking out what was growing in the farms nearby. Apples, plums, crab apples, saskatoons, strawberries and raspberries began to appear on the dinner table. Freezers were brought into the basement of the farmhouse for the extras and lined up with their own generators keeping them cold.

A cold room was also built in the basement, insulated to keep the temperature low and vented to the outside to let in fresh air. A large thermometer was mounted on the wall to warn whenever the room was getting too cold, necessitating a closure of the vents. Shelves were already lined with jars of fruit and vegetables as well as a collection of a variety of jams, jellies, pickles and relishes. Near the back a whole section was dedicated to the lard that had been rendered from the two hogs that had been butchered in September. Bins had been built and were waiting for the potatoes, carrots, beets and cabbages that would soon fill them.

It was Susie who suggested that they have a feast to celebrate all of the food that they had put away for the winter months. She was standing in the cold cellar, handing jars of jelly to her mother to line up on the shelves when she said "We're kind of like the pilgrims aren't we. But we didn't need the Indians to help us. We did it all on our own. We need to celebrate."

Thanksgiving seemed to be the perfect time to do this, and so the plan was put into action. Everyone in the group except the Bergman's had been busy during the week creating a special dish to share at the feast. And now it was their turn as they roasted the four turkeys, complete with four different kinds of stuffing: a favourite from the Burdocks, the Reese's. the James and, of course the Bergmans, themselves. The kitchen smelled heavenly!

As they gathered around the table that afternoon, each family presented the dish that they had prepared, and shared a little story about what it meant to their family, and why they had chosen it for the feast. The last to arrive were the platters with the four turkeys which were set down at equal distances on the tables. A set of carving tools was handed to the person sitting directly in front of each turkey by the Bergman children.

"Help!" cried Bradley. I've never done anything like this before."

"Ah, the joys of random seating! I'm not worried," said his mother. "You can do it."

Everyone laughed as Jim thrust the fork into the turkey before him. "I'm sure you can't do any worse than me." He sliced off a piece of the breast and slid it onto April's plate beside his. "Here you go girl. Let the feasting begin."

For some time, the only sounds that one could hear in the yard were those of eating: the pouring of water, the clink of cutlery on the china plates and the soft murmur of please pass the buns. In time, they set aside their utensils., one by one, truly satiated. A feel of contentment swept through the group as they sat looking at each other with smiles on their faces. And then, in the true spirit of thanksgiving, members of the group began to share what they were grateful for.

Margret was the last to speak "As I listen to you all, I can't help but think back to that afternoon when Frank and Jim showed up at my house. I was waiting for my husband John to come. I was so angry when Joelle let them in. Well, maybe angry is not the right word as much as scared. Then there was that drive out of the city. It was so empty, so quiet. I didn't know where we were going, and I didn't know what was going to happen to us. I was so afraid. Now look at us. Look at what we have accomplished in less than a year. It's utterly remarkable. I feel truly at home, and I have all of you to thank for that. Together you have given me and my girls, life beyond measure. Thank you so much."

"My grandmother was an avid fan of Jimi Hendrix. She would often quote his words to me. One of her favourite lines was 'when the power of love overcomes the love of power, the world will have peace.' I can still hear her muttering that to the television when she was watching the news. She knew that there was a way to achieve peace, but she also was a realist. She was aware that giving up the love of power was an impossibility for most people. As I sat at this table today and look around at each of you, I realize that we seem to have achieved that impossibility. The love of power between us is no more. The power of love, of cooperation and of consensus has taken over. For that I am truly grateful."

Lucy was fuming as she stomped across the yard to Margret's RV. She pounded on the door. She didn't even wait for Margret to say good morning when she opened it. She screamed out "How dare you let your slut of a daughter seduce my son!"

Margret was taken completely aback. She had been sitting at the table enjoying her morning coffee when the pounding started and moved very quickly to open the door, expecting that something had happened to either Marisa or Joelle. Instead the word slut had hit her like a bolt out of the blue. She screamed back "How dare you call my daughter a slut!"

In the meantime, Trevor was on a full run to the house to get Jim and Frank. He burst into the kitchen without knocking and cried out. "You've got to come. I can take care of Lucy, but someone has to look after Margret."

Both men immediately rose to their feet as Jim cried out, "What's wrong with Margret?"

"I'll explain it on the way," Trevor gasped as he turned and headed out the door. Both men followed. Across the yard they could see the two women screaming at each other on the step leading into Margret's RV.

"Bill surprised us with an announcement at breakfast this morning," Trevor explained as he ran. "He told us that he and Joelle are planning to move into the RV that has been standing empty since Stan and his family left and start their own family. Well, Lucy is on the warpath. She thinks that Bill is far too young to take a step like this and she is blaming everything on Margret. I tried to talk some sense into her, but she took off before I could stop her." By now Trevor was unable to speak as he huffed with exertion. As the men neared the women, they could hear the fight clearly.

Margret screamed," My daughter didn't seduce your son. She's the minor in this situation."

"Well just look at you." Lucy responded. "Anyone can see that you are making a good example for your daughters. You taught them well."

"That's enough Lucy!" Trevor exclaimed as he reached his wife. He picked her up and threw her over his shoulder in the fireman's hold and carried her kicking and screaming back to their trailer.

Jim ran up the steps and wrapped Margret in his arms as Frank looked into the window of the RV. Joelle was standing there, looking out, with tears running down her face. "Jim," he called out. "We have to look after her too," as he nodded his head towards the window.

Jim glanced in the window and then gently pushed Margret inside. "Joelle heard it all," he whispered.

Margret turned to look at Joelle and then rushed to hold her in her arms. "Oh, my poor baby. You didn't need to hear that."

"I was going to tell you this morning Mom. We were so excited and now look at this mess."

"It's not so bad, baby. It's just a knee jerk reaction when you first learn something like this. Lucy is being a mother. She'll be okay when she gets used to the idea. We just have to give her a little time."

"But what about you? Why aren't you having a knee jerk reaction?"

"Well, I've known there was something going on between you and Bill for some time now. She looked over Joelle's head and mouthed 'thank you' to Jim."

"How did you know? We've kept it so secret."

"I'm your mama, baby. You'll understand when you become a mama."

"Are you upset with us?"

"No, not now. I was in the beginning because you are so young. I wanted you to experience so many other things before you settled down with a man. Just like Lucy wants for Bill. But then I realized I was stuck in a dream world. I was treating our life here like it was something like summer camp, and the day would come when we would all return to our old life and you could resume doing all the things I wanted. When I realized that this was impossible, I accepted the inevitable. This is your life now. Yours and Bill's. You will make the decisions together that will work for you. All that other stuff doesn't exist anymore."

"Thank you, Mama. I think I am going to go and lie down now." She hugged her mother tightly, kissed her cheek and ambled towards the back of the RV.

Margret sat down at the table and slumped forward, her head on her arms. "Is this what is going to be like for my baby? Is she going to have to listen to people calling her mother a slut?"

Jim sat down beside and stroked her hair. "I don't know my darling. It's not about what others think. It's about who you truly know you are inside."

Frank sat across from them. "You know you aren't a slut Margret. No one who truly knows you will ever say that. I'm pretty certain Lucy doesn't even think that. It was all said in the heat of the moment."

"I know you're right." Margret lifted her head. "It's just hard in the moment. I know this baby is going to have to face things my girls never did."

She turned and looked at Jim. "I'm so glad that you were there for me when I found out, Jim. At least you stopped me from making a fool of myself like Lucy did. Not that my reaction was much better than hers today, was it?"

Jim slipped his arm around her shoulders and pulled her close to him. "Just glad I could be of service, my dear!"

Frank got up and said, "It looks like you have everything under control here. I think I'll go and see how Trevor and Lucy are getting on."

About a half hour later, there was another knock on the door. It was Bill. "Joelle and I were planning on going in the city today to get a few things. We want to fix up Stan's RV before we move in to make it ours. You don't mind, do you?"

"Not at all."

"Well, is she ready?"

"I'm not sure. Joelle," she called out, "Bill's here."

"Coming," came the voice from the back room.

Jim and Margret stood in the doorway together, their arms around each other's waists, watching the youngsters drive away.

"I think it's time for you to move in with me," he murmured.

"Before the baby is born?"

"Why not? It won't be that long, and it might be good to be settled before you have to start all those night feedings. Besides, I want you to."

"Well, give me a little time. You may be right about settling in. I'll have to think about it."

"Are you okay? I hate to rush away but Adam is bringing the plans over for the renovation of the downstairs of the house. He thinks we should make it an open concept so that all of us can fit in more comfortably now that winter is coming. This Indian summer isn't going to last forever."

"I'm fine. Actually, I am very fine, much, much better than I would have been after a scene like this a year ago. I guess I am finally beginning to mature."

As Margret turned to go back into her home her mind swept back to the first apartment she and John had shared so many years before. She remembered all the feelings that went with creating a new home; the excitement, the anticipation and even more so the trepidation that she might do everything wrong. And now it was Joelle's turn to make a home with Bill. The world might not be quite the same as it was when she was a newlywed, but she was sure that her daughter would still experience many of those same feelings.

The next morning Lucy was back at Margret's door again, this time with a very contrite face. Her knock was soft and her voice quiet when Margret opened the door and stood looking out at her.

"I came to apologize, Margret, I am so sorry for everything I said yesterday. I would have brought you a big bouquet of flowers if I could have, but I hear the delivery trucks aren't running. I just hope you will forgive me; not that I deserve it."

"Come on in. I just made up a pot of herbal tea. I'd love to share it with you?"

"You would? I'm not sure that I would be so gracious if I was in your shoes."

"Well, it's not really about being gracious. You see, I was in your shoes a while back when I first learned about Bill and Joelle. I nearly caused a bigger scene than you did yesterday. In fact, I would have, hadn't Jim been there to stop me. The only difference is that I was going after Bill, not you. I understand completely where you were coming from. You were just being a mama bear looking after her first born."

"Thank you for that. I guess it's a good thing to have a man around when the extreme mother instinct swings into gear."

I couldn't believe how easily Trevor threw you over his shoulder and walked away."

"It's his fireman training. Something people don't think of when they are dealing with a banker. I was so angry and then absolutely mortified realizing that the whole group was watching my husband pack me off like that. I'm sure it gave everyone a good laugh."

"Well, maybe not yesterday, but I'm sure it's something we will look back and chuckle at now and then in the years to come."

"A story to share with our grandchildren perhaps."

"Perhaps."

That evening Margret stood up during the group meeting and said she had something to share. She started by saying that she hoped that she and Lucy had not made everyone too uncomfortable as they were working out their angst in public as mothers. She also apologized to Bill and Joelle for their embarrassment and wished them all the best in their new home. Lucy followed suit.

However, she continued on, she had spent a lot of time in deep thought since the encounter with Lucy. She wanted everyone to know that she had forgiven Lucy for everything she had said, because she knew perfectly well it was said without thought. In the midst of that, she had decided that she needed to come clean about the baby she was carrying.

"Frank and I decided that we didn't need to share this story back in April when we first arrived on the farm because it doesn't concern any of you. And while that is true, it does concern this baby, who is going to be part of our community, most likely for the rest of his or her life. I know you are all wondering about how I got pregnant, even if you are too polite to say anything. Yesterday I realized that I can either share with you what happened to me, or this baby can have people in its life wondering and perhaps whispering about it. Secrets take a lot of energy. Tonight, I want to tell you what happened so, at least in the future, my child can hear the real story from everyone, not what people have conjured up in their minds because they never knew the truth."

Margret went on to tell what had happened to her on the day of the storm. She omitted certain details in much the same way she had with her daughters, but this time when Lucy gasped, "You were raped!"

She shook her head and said "No, not really. I don't want my child to think it was a result of rape. I was far more concerned about the safety of my daughters that day than I was about myself. I responded in the way I had to respond, in order to keep them safe. So, I can't claim it was rape."

"Where is the father then?" asked Samuel. "Why isn't he here with us now?"

Frank responded to the question. "I went to look for him when Margret told me what had happened. He was dead. We're not sure why. I don't think it was the flu. Perhaps he killed himself. He obviously was suffering from cabin fever, what with his talk of Adam and Eve and so on."

Everyone sat and looked at the floor for a few minutes. Finally, Lucy broke the silence. "I find it fascinating how quiet we all become when we are faced with the reality of life like this. It's like we all have to examine our own souls."

She turned to Margret and said, "Thank you for sharing your story. I have to admit I was wondering and I want to apologize again for the words I used yesterday."

Margret reached over and squeezed her hand. "It's okay, but if you ever do it again, I'll have to throw you over my shoulder and cart you away myself."

Everyone laughed, as the tension was broken.

"And now," Margret turned to Jim, "I do believe that you and Adam have a major renovation idea that you would like to share with us."

37

Jim stood at his regular spot at the kitchen window while his coffee was brewing, looking out over the east pasture. He thought back to the day that he decided that he would spread Julie's ashes there so that she could continue to enjoy the sun as it rose. He had never gotten around to doing it. He wondered if her ashes were still at the funeral home. Would he find them if he made the effort to look? Maybe David or Patrick would know. He would have to ask them. He frowned slightly as he looked to the east. The sun sure looked different this morning.

It had been an easy winter compared to the one they had gone through the previous year. The days of Indian Summer they had enjoyed at Thanksgiving continued on throughout the rest of the month, providing lots of time to prepare the motor homes as well as the buildings for the livestock for the winter. November was a bit colder, but the first snow didn't fall until mid-December, diminishing the need to deal with it by several weeks. By the end of January, Jim noticed that the rabbits were already turning brown, a sure sign that there wouldn't be any more snow. And there wasn't. Although the spring temperatures didn't arrive until the beginning of March, no more snow had fallen.

Winter had become a time of learning for everyone in the group. Although Connie Reese was a teacher and could have taken over and taught all the children at once in a one room school, it was decided that everyone should become a teacher and work with the children from time to time. Textbooks were harvested from the schools in the city and school supplies of all kinds were brought out from the Staples store. The plan was simple. Each person chose what they wanted to teach each month and at what level. By the end of the winter every adult had the opportunity to work with each of the children at least once.

Most of their research for these studies took place in the libraries in the city: the public library as well as the one in the college. In the beginning there was a lot of grumbling about how much easier it would be if they could access the internet, but in time they all adjusted to the reality of working with books again.

Jim had to admit that it had been a good plan in the long run. Everyone was kept busy. There was no time to dwell on the lives they had lived before the virus had ripped their lives apart. All of the children had developed good relationships with each of the adults in their own unique way. Margret claimed that her grandmother had always lived with the premise that a child can never have too many people loving them. Well, it certainly looked like it was true for these children. They were all loved in ways that he could never have imagined last year at this time.

Margret's baby had been born on Christmas Eve. It was a beautiful little boy that she named Jonathon. She explained to the group that her grandmother had never believed that children should have the same first name as anyone else in a family. Having their own unique name gave them the opportunity to develop their personality free from having to live up to expectations based on the life of the person who had gone before. She didn't know for certain if this was true but thought it couldn't hurt to follow her grandmother's advice. And so, in the end, he was called Jonathon Ashton, after his father John. Everyone smiled and nodded when she said this. They gathered the baby into their arms and loved him unconditionally, in much the same way as they did all the other children.

His coffee was ready. Jim poured himself a cup and went out to the veranda to drink it. The warm dry winds that had been blowing all month were still rushing past the house. "March winds, April showers," he muttered, "bring May flowers. I sure would prefer some of those showers this April". Not a drop of rain had fallen all month.

He walked to the far corner of the veranda where the side wall would provide some protection from the wind. He was about to sink down onto the swing, when he glanced at the rising sun again. There was something odd going on. It shouldn't take this long to come over the horizon. And then a realization struck him. It wasn't the sun. It was a fire. Grande Prairie was burning up.

Jim stood staring at the horizon in horror. Now that he had realized that it was a fire, he could also see how big it was. Most of the city appeared to be in flames and there wasn't a thing he could do about it. Suddenly there was a large boom and the flames leapt high into the sky. "Probably a propane tank," called out Trevor as he came across the yard. "A big one by the looks of that blast." "So, what are we going to do?" asked Jim.

"What can we do? We don't have water bombers or water pressure or anything that one needs to fight a fire, especially of that size. We're just going to have to let in burn."

"That seems rather hopeless."

"Well, if you have any ideas, I wouldn't mind hearing them; but, with these winds and everything that's sitting there, just waiting to blow up, I would prefer to stay right here where it's safe."

"At least the wind is blowing from the south west right now, so we are safe. But if it turns, it could head in this direction. You know how wild it has been these last few weeks." Frank ambled down the steps as he talked.

Another explosion occurred, not quite as loud as the last one.

"It's obviously not safe to go in there" said Paul. "We aren't prepared for anything like this." By now everyone was gathering in front of the house, staring at the fire.

"Between the wind, the lack of moisture and all that dry, unmown grass from last summer, it's a real tinderbox." "I wonder how it started? We haven't had any lightning lately, have we?"

"Not that I noticed."

"What about the guys in the mall? Has anyone seen them this spring?"

"No, but they should have made it through this winter if they managed to survive last year. It was far worse last year."

"We have got to go in and find them!" exclaimed Patrick.

Another explosion ripped through the city: a blast so strong that the windows in the house rattled.

"Wow! There sure are a lot of explosions. What's blowing up?" Alan had joined the group.

"Could be a number of different things," Trevor replied. "Propane bottles for certain, there's one on every patio with a barbecue. There are a number of propane filling stations throughout the city with the large tanks which will likely go. And then there are the gas tanks on cars, the oxygen tanks used by those with lung problems, dynamite, gun powder, acetylene cylinders and even fertilizers. The list goes on and on. We didn't live in the safest world when it came to explosive material."

"Even hair spray will blow if it gets hot enough."

"Yes, anything that is pressurized has to be added to the list. Helium, for example, is non-combustible, but the tanks used to fill the balloons will explode when heated. I expect it's all in there somewhere. Our main problem is not knowing what and where. We could be killed or seriously injured by flying shrapnel at any moment."

"What about the fuel that's sitting below ground? Will those tanks blow?"

"Well they shouldn't if they are sealed tight. But if the flames can get in, they will. The problem is the pumps. If they burn, they open up the tanks to the flames. The fuller the tank, the safer it is. It's the gas that forms in the empty space that is the most dangerous."

"We have practically drained a few of them already."

"Yes, they're the ones I'm worried about. Let's just hope the pumps are far enough from any building to catch fire.

"I don't think we have answered the most important question," said Patrick. "I realize we can't fight the fire, but do we risk our lives going into the centre of the city to rescue three men who may not even be there anymore?"

There was an uncomfortable silence as the men pondered the situation. Finally, Alan spoke up. "Somehow this doesn't feel like a group consensus decision. It's more of an individual choice. If anyone wants to go, they can. But if you don't, it's okay."

Jim's eyes met Frank's across the crowd. He shrugged his shoulders and ran his fingers through his hair. "Well I, for one, can't let them die without trying to save them. It may be crazy, but at least I want to check the mall where they were living."

"You know I'm with you," said Frank.

"Me too," said Paul as a number of voices also joined in stating their desire to look for the men."

"Well, we don't need to all go," said Jim. "There's no need for all of us to risk our lives. After all there are only three of them. We know where they sleep. And we know that they pretty well stick together all the time."

"So, who's it going to be?" asked Darren.

"I think it should be me," Paul replied. "After all, I am an EMT and have the training."

"I'd like to go too, said Trevor. "I was a volunteer fireman for a few years, so I have some training. I also developed a bit of a friendship over the past year with those old men.

Whenever I ran into them when I was in the city, we would sit and talk for a while. I think they trust me."

"Is that okay with the rest of you?" asked Jim?

A chorus of assents started slowly as each considered the reality of sending one of the group into danger. Jim waited patiently until everyone had agreed before he continued. "So that's decided then. We can't leave the men to burn, if we can help it. Paul and Trevor are going to look for them. You can take my crew cab. You will need the extra room if you find them."

"You had better not go without breakfast." Margret called out as she went up the steps to the house. "If someone will bring me the eggs from the hen house, I'll scramble up a batch."

Margret had just set the plates of steaming eggs in front of Paul and Trevor when Caleb and Jacob burst through the kitchen door. "Come quick! There's someone coming up the driveway."

Breakfast was forgotten for the moment as they all rushed out to see who was coming. A lone man was staggering down the driveway, holding out his hands towards them beseechingly. As he got closer, Trevor peered down the road and then said "I recognize him. It's Albert Butler. He's one of the men from the mall."

Albert's voice was raspy as he cried out, "I tried to save them. I really did, but the flames were too fierce."

Trevor and Paul rushed to him and helped him make his way up the rest of the driveway. They brought him into the kitchen and pulled out a chair for him at the table. When he saw the eggs, his face brightened and asked,

"May I?"

"Certainly," said Margret. She smiled at Paul and said "There's lots. I'll get you another plate."

As he sat there, shoveling the eggs into his mouth, the rest of the group silently took stock of his condition. He was dirty and disheveled with clothes that appeared to have been slept in. His hands and face were blackened with smoke. Contrasting white lines ran down each cheek from tears recently shed.

Margret set a cup of coffee before him. He mixed in four tablespoons of sugar and then filled the cup to the brim with cream before he took a sip. His eyes closed in ecstasy and he began to speak. "Thank you. I haven't had a hot coffee for so long."

Jim was the first to respond. "The fire. What happened?" he asked in a gentle voice.

"I don't know, I just woke up smelling smoke, and when I looked out the window the whole motel was ablaze." He went on to tell a rambling story of a fight he had had the night before with his buddies about money. They had taken to trying out different motels in the city once spring arrived, just for the fun of it. Last night they were staying at the Thrift lodge -- not fancy, but more to their liking than any of the other places they had tried out so far. They were sitting in the lawn chairs by the door sharing a bottle of rum. Mickey brought up the issue of still waiting to be paid for the damage to his back by Workman's Compensation. Ernest had joined in, supporting him by running down the insurance industry for making people wait so long. In the meantime, he had told them not to be so stupid, that there was no one left to pay them anything, and even if there was, what good was money these days anyway. Well, the fight was on and it got louder and louder and even more ridiculous. Finally, Mickey got up and took a swing at him. He decided this wasn't worth it and crossed the parking lot to stay in a room there for the night. He fell asleep listening to them through the open window congratulating each other for winning the argument.

"It was the smoke that woke me up. It had filled the whole room. When I got outside the west side of the motel was completely covered in flames. I broke down the door of their room and went inside. I couldn't wake them up. I couldn't. They wouldn't open their eyes. The flames were so hot and I, I had to leave, it just was too hot. I couldn't do it." He began to sob.

Margret picked up a box of Kleenex and brought it over to the table. As she handed it to Albert, she began softly stroking his back. He gradually relaxed and continued on with his story.

"Once I realized I needed help, I thought of you all. Started walking, hoping to find you. I knew you were out here somewhere, but not exactly where. Thank goodness for that sign on the highway. I've been walking all night." Tears started running down his face again creating more streaks on his face.

"I wonder how it started?" asked Frank.

"Probably cigarettes," Albert mumbled behind the tissue he was dabbing his nose with. "Ernest had this terrible habit of smoking in bed. I was constantly putting out his butts after he had fallen asleep. But I wasn't there last night to do it. I told him. I told him so many times, but he just wouldn't listen. And now look at the mess he made."

A deep sense of futility hung over everyone in the room, as they listened to Albert. This futility ruled their emotions for the next two weeks as the fire continued to burn. The fire was the first thought in each mind every morning and the last as they closed their eyes in sleep. Although they tried not to think about it, most of their energy was spent watching and waiting, feeling more helpless than they had ever felt before.

Jim pulled out the tractor and cultivator and created a fire break along the whole length of the east pasture. He was heartsick at wiping out the grass just as it was beginning to grow but he had to do something. Would it be enough to stop the flames? He wasn't sure. It would all depend on how strong the wind was and which direction it was coming from.

The wind, itself, was relentless, blasting the house from one direction after another, day after day after day. There were times that the glow of the fire seemed to disappear from the sky, providing a faint hope that it was extinguished. However, in no time at all, it seemed, the wind swept the flames into life again. If it wasn't the wind, it was the explosions. Their dull thuds filled the air from time to time as tanks and cylinders succumbed to the force of the intense heat, spreading the flames in new directions.

Rain finally arrived on the fifth of May. It was only a sprinkle, but it was enough to provide a sliver of hope. Disappointment reigned the next morning when they awoke to clear blue skies. Thankfully, the clouds returned the next day. The rain pounded the dry earth for two solid days before it stopped. The fire was over. The farm was safe.

On the 10th of May Jim found a note lying on the kitchen table. It was from Albert. He wrote that he appreciated everything that the group had done for him in the past month, but he was sorry. He just wasn't comfortable being surrounded by so many people all the time. A couple, like Mickey and Ernest had been okay, but forty at a time was just too much. He was going to head west, walk to Wembley or maybe Beaverlodge and continue to live his life there. He hoped Jim and the others would understand.

38

Jim and Margret were sitting on the verandah gazing up at the Milky Way. "Isn't it beautiful," Margret said in a dreamy voice. "It's kind of hard to believe that I lived most of my life without having a clue how many stars are up there. I could see the big dipper and Orion on occasion, but nothing like this."

"It's one of the joys of not having a steady stream of electricity coming at us."

"So true, but now I find I just take them for granted most of the time. I should be sitting out here every night looking at them. They give one such a sense of peace; of being connected to the whole universe."

Jonathon stirred in his sleep on the swing beside them. They both looked at him for a moment and then turned back to the sky. "He's beat," Margret murmured. "It's been a pretty exciting day for him."

"For all of us. It went well, didn't it."

"Yes, it did. It was so good to have a real Thanksgiving to celebrate this year."

"Remember the first one. Now that was a feast!"

"We were so proud of everything we had accomplished together."

"It's hard to believe that it was five years ago already. Things got a lot harder after that. First there was the year of the fire and the drought. We couldn't get anything to grow, no matter how hard we tried. Had to rely that winter on what was left over from the year before and what was still in the bins."

"It almost wiped us out, didn't it? Used up all the seeds we had collected with nothing to show for them. If we hadn't had the livestock and all those dry goods that you insisted we salvage to pull us through, we wouldn't have made it."

"Thankfully Teresa thought about your grandmother getting the parcels of seeds in the mail during our third winter. Checking out the back rooms in the rural post offices provided us with more. We found enough seeds to get us through that summer."

"At least that whole experience taught us the importance of drying seeds for the next year's garden. We lost quite a few of them with our first attempts but we continued to learn. This year's harvest proved that we can succeed."

"That was also the year of the accident, wasn't it?"

"Horrible!" Margret murmured, shaking her head as the memories flooded her mind. "Losing the boys was absolutely heartbreaking for all of us. Wherever they got the idea that they should take Marisa's Mustang for a joyride was beyond me. High speeds and loose gravel are nothing to fool around with. Caleb, Lester, Todd and Toby all gone in an instant. It was absolutely devastating."

"Grief to the nth degree. I wondered, at times, if their parents were going to pull through. It certainly reminded me of everything we lost in the beginning. Even I was beginning to wonder what we were trying to accomplish."

"The crazy thing is that, in the midst of the grief, one can't stop living no matter how much you want to. You may want to throw up your hands and quit, but you can't. You keep on striving, no matter how hard it is or how much it hurts."

"I think Alan and Linda had given up, a least for a while. That's where the community became so important. The rest of us could take over for a time."

"Yes, in the end, it's your friends and the children you still have that pull you through."

They both sighed deeply.

The silence of the evening was interrupted by a shrill neigh which brought Jim's gaze down from the sky to survey the farmyard spread out before them. So much had changed over the years. Frank had moved back to the home he had grown up in, on the quarter section to the south, taking Lily and her children with him. Samuel and his family had moved across the road and were living in Julie's parent's home. The younger couples: Marisa and Paul, Joelle and Bill, Marcy and Patrick and Kelly and David had taken over the empty motor homes, moving them together to create living spaces double in size, which made the area by the dugout look much less like a mobile home park from the past. A community centre with a large kitchen and dining rom had been built by garden, giving Jim and Margret privacy in the original farmhouse. Next too it, the corrals for the horses had been constructed.

It took almost four years for the gasoline stored underground to begin to break down. Once it was no longer dependable in the vehicles, horses had not only become the main source of transportation. but also depended upon for most of the farm work. In the midst of moving forward as a community, Jim knew they were also moving backwards. He was pondering the question of whether there will ever come a time when humanity would get back to where they were before this all happened.

His thoughts were interrupted by Margret's voice beside him, softly saying. "The next two years weren't as bad, were they? Everything seemed to get a little bit easier."

"The weather certainly was better, not only during the growing season; but, also throughout winter."

"It sure made a difference. The garden was top notch this year. And the berries! The bushes were covered."

"Hence today's feast. It was good wasn't it."

"Yes, and wasn't Samuel funny when he was trying to help catch the turkeys?"

"Well, at least he was trying to face his fears, though I do think he actually made it more difficult for the rest of us in the long run. "

"And it was even funnier when the children decided to play the turkey game they had created and insisted he be the turkey! I haven't laughed so hard in ages. He's such a good sport!"

"That he is. Five years! Well five and a half if one counts when it all started. It feels like forever."

"When I think about our days in Minneapolis it is almost like reading a fairy tale. Once upon a time, you know."

"The same here. Once upon a time I went to Brazil to convince the cattlemen of the world how important I was. I haven't got a clue who that man was anymore and yet, at the same time I do know it was me."

"What was that? Did you feel it?"

"It felt weird. Like the ground was moving".

"Look," Margret gestured towards the hanging baskets that decorated the front entry. "The plants are swaying. Do you think it was an earthquake?"

"As far as I understand, we don't have earthquakes in Alberta."

"I think there was talk of some when I was a child. They were way up in Alaska, though. Nothing to worry about. But people said they felt them."

"There it is again. Feels stronger this time. Even the swing is swaying now."

"We had better put Jonathon in his bed before this wakes him up."

They both stood up. Margret held the door open as Jim scooped Jonathon up in his arms. Together they ascended the stairs to the bedroom. Margret pulled back the blankets on the boy's bed and Jim carefully laid him down, so as not to wake him. She kissed his cheek softly as she tucked the blankets around him. "Sleep well my little man," she murmured.

She turned back to Jim and reached for his hand. "And now, my big man, let's go to bed. I think we may have a little more celebrating to do."

EPILOGUE

Joseph Russell urged his horse up the steep incline with one hand holding the reins, and the other the small boy seated in the saddle in front of him. His life had changed dramatically since he made this journey with his grandfather so many years ago. At that point he was living what his people called a "white" life, with school, cars, television and electricity. However, all of that was left behind when he was a teen.

The social fabric of the Tsay Keh Dene people had deteriorated after the dam was completed. In less than ten years his grandfather decided to return to the world of his ancestors to save his family. Three other families chose to go with them. They sold all their vehicles, replacing them with horses, and headed into the wilderness to live. Every spring they returned to the community to cash their treaty cheques and stock up on flour, sugar, tobacco, tea and ammunition. The rest of the year they lived off the land as their people had done before them for countless generations.

This pattern had changed slightly five years ago when they arrived at the Ingenika trading post and discovered that there was no one there. They took the supplies that they needed and returned to the forest without having any idea that a virus had wiped out, not only the rest of their people, but also most of the world. They hadn't returned since.

Although Joe was usually very comfortable on horseback, he was slightly uneasy riding into this territory on this day with his precious grandson. An earthquake had rumbled through the area a week before. He didn't want to have to deal with unexpected landslides or cervices beneath the feet of his horse. However, it was the child's fifth birthday, and the handing on of the lessons of his people, could not be ignored.

They made it safely to the top of the hill and dismounted, tying the reins of the horse to a small alder. Together they walked to edge of the cliff, in much the same way that he had done with his own grandfather. He reached out to hold his grandson's hand as they reached the precipice. The lake spread out before them as far as their eyes could see.

Joseph began to speak. He told his grandson of the trees that he had seen as a child and pointed to the dam that had changed everything. He repeated the words of his grandfather, describing how their land had been stolen from them to provide electricity for the rest of the people. He shared the importance of taking care of this beautiful world with all of the gifts it provides. He talked of their people, a strong people who had lived on this land for more years than anyone can remember. He, in turn, promised to pass on to this child the tools that his grandfather had given him over the years. When his speech was complete, they stood in silence together looking out over the lake. Finally, they turned and walked back to where the horse was tethered.

As they rode down into the valley, portions of the dam began to crumble. Little streams of water began to trickle through the openings. Suddenly with a mighty roar, the whole dam collapsed. A wall of water swept eastward down the Peace River: a wall of water that would, in very little time, cover one third of northern Alberta, drowning everything in its path.

The end.

Thank you for completing *Consequences.*

We would love if you could help by posting a review at your book retailer and on the PageMaster Publishing site. It only takes a minute and it would really help others by giving them an idea of your experience.

Thanks

PM Store Author's QR Code
https://pagemasterpublishing.ca/by/gail-gillingham/

To order more copies of this book, find books by other Canadian authors, or make inquiries about publishing your own book, contact PageMaster at:

PageMaster Publication Services Inc.
11340-120 Street, Edmonton, AB T5G 0W5
books@pagemaster.ca
780-425-9303

catalogue and e-commerce store
PageMasterPublishing.ca/Shop

About the Author

GAIL GILLINGHAM WYLIE is Canadian mother, grandmother and great grandmother who has always wanted to be a writer, in the midst of not finding the time to do so. As a history major in university, she was always fascinated by the archeological findings of the past that indicate there was much more going on back then, than we have a tendency to recognize. This led to questioning how much of our present world would survive if a catastrophe of some sort wiped out the majority of humanity. For fifty plus years she worked on this question in her mind, pulling together thoughts, facts and story plots in the midst of her busy life. In 2018 she finally had the time to put all of the details she had gathered over the years onto paper. Consequences is her final attempt to answer this question in the form of a novel.

Gail currently lives near Edmonton, Alberta with her husband Clay. In the midst of their retirement, they also work together work using Quantum Biofeedback as a tool to allow the human body to heal itself. Gail has a BA in psychology and a MSc in Individual, Marital and Family Therapy. She was a stay home mother and foster parent while her sons were growing up. She worked as a family therapist focusing on autism from the late eighties on, writing and publishing books on this topic as well as traveling the world speaking at conferences and working directly with families, schools and day services providers, teaching them what she learned from those on the spectrum.

At present, Gail is enjoying having the time to write for pleasure of writing. Who knows – there may be more novels coming out in the future.